Rating YOUR Bunkmates

» AND OTHER CAMP CRIMES «

For Mom and Dad

Rating Your Bunkmates and Other Camp Crimes is published by Capstone Editions, an imprint of Capstone.
1710 Roe Crest Drive
North Mankato, Minnesota 56003
www.capstonepub.com

Library of Congress Cataloging-in-Publication Data is available on the Library of Congress website.

ISBN 978-1-68446-077-9 (hardcover)
ISBN 978-1-68446-078-6 (eBook PDF)

Summary: Twelve-year-old Abigail Hensley is a socially awkward aspiring anthropologist who has always had trouble connecting with her peers. Abigail is hopeful that a week at sleepaway camp is the answer to finally making a friend. After all, her extensive research shows that summer camp is the best place to make lifelong connections. Using her tried-and-true research methods, Abigail begins to study her cabinmates for friendship potential. But just when it seems that she is off to a good start, her bunkmate's phone gets stolen, and Abigail is the main suspect. Can she clear her name, find the real culprit, and make a friend before the week is done?

Image Credits
author photo—Amy Wright

Editorial Credits
Designed by Brann Garvey
Illustrations by Alexandra Bye

Printed and bound in the United States of America.
003075

Rating YOUR Bunkmates

AND OTHER CAMP CRIMES

by Jennifer Orr

CAPSTONE EDITIONS
a capstone imprint

FIELD NOTES

> ## Date and Time:
> Sunday, June 26, 9:47 a.m.
>
> ## Location:
> Somewhere on Highway 101

Description of Activity:

Propulsion toward either crowning achievement or inescapable calamity. For the first time ever, I'm going to summer camp. Mom predicts success. She cranes her neck around the passenger's seat headrest and recites all the benefits of sleepaway camp—fireside sing-alongs, collaborative games, cozy cabins. "All designed to promote healthy girl bonding," she says.

Dad points out the scientific merits of camp: quiet hikes for studying nature, a rugged environment similar to that of an archaeological dig, and food cooked over an open flame. He catches my eye in the rearview mirror and says, "Like one giant Bunsen burner, Abigail."

As my parents chat about their own fond memories of summer camp, I begin writing field notes to document my experiences over the next week. Like a real anthropologist, a scientist who studies people, I plan to use these notes to help me with my ongoing experiment: finding a friend.

Reflections:

I appreciate my parents' sunny attitudes. They are my biggest cheerleaders in all my endeavors, both scientific and social. I, too, am trying to keep a positive outlook on my upcoming week at Camp Hollyhock. Despite research that shows that my age—twelve—is the optimal age for camp,[1] I'm worried my attempts to forge yet another friendship could easily mimic the results of past experiments . . . complete and utter failure. No matter how hard I try, I can't seem to successfully befriend a girl my age. It's like I'm helium, physically unable to mix with any other chemical element. Bonding with girls my age just doesn't seem part of my atomic makeup.

Evidence of my inability to make friends first emerged seven years ago, during the Playdate Experiment. I brought my favorite rocks to a playdate Mom had arranged with a girl from my kindergarten class. Lainey suggested we build fairy houses with my rocks. I told her fairies didn't exist. She said they did. Like any good scientist, I demanded proof. She pulled out some treasures the fairies had left under her pillow. I examined them closely, borrowing Lainey's magnifying glass for precise study. On the miniature "fairy wand," I pointed out a small engraving in the wood. *Made in China.* Lainey collapsed into tears, and I was never invited back.

Shortly after this experiment, I was moved up to the first grade. At the end of the school year, my teacher recommended that I skip second grade completely. Experiencing the third grade as a six-year-old wasn't a successful social experiment. Neither was the year I left behind my elementary peers and skipped straight to middle school, where all my requests for playdates were declined with hysterical laughter.

Other disastrous friend experiments include:

1.) Mother-Daughter Book Club:

Apparently the *book* part of this club was merely a suggestion. I presented a thoughtful twenty-minute slideshow presentation on Madeleine L'Engle's *A Wrinkle in Time*. Nobody, except for Mom, who is always up for a lively debate on time travel, seemed interested in discussing the book—or anything else, for that matter—with me.

2.) Bay Area Fencing Ice Cream Social:

As an avid fencer, I had high hopes for this event. But while I was enjoying a perfect spoonful of whipped cream, chocolate sauce, and ice cream, Lola Brown asked me to show her my lunging techniques. Astonished, I swallowed the frozen treat too quickly, resulting in sphenopalatine ganglioneuralgia.[2] Through the searing head pain, I managed to tell her, "Absolutely not." What if she used my moves against me in a future match? The social coordinator laughed off my report that Lola was a possible spy, and I was forced to take my ice cream to go. I'm not sure how friendly you can be with someone you will eventually fight with a saber, anyway.

Reflections, continued:

Though these results are disappointing, I continue with my efforts. I don't want to end up like helium, so self-satisfied with my full shell of electrons that I don't need to bond with any other element. Floating by yourself forever seems quite sad and lonely. Since I don't wish this type of existence for myself, I carry on with my experiments. After all, that's what we do in science.

Change the variables. See how the results will change. This time, I'm changing the environment.

My educational environment has never been adequate for making friends. Because I skipped three grades, I now attend the local high school instead of the middle school. At first I thought I would be able to bond with these older students because my social interests are as advanced as my academic ones. But alas, I have been unable to find high-school students who enjoy discussing anthropology, time travel, or French cuisine.

So I had to start looking elsewhere. My research shows that summer camp might be a more ideal place for me to meet lifelong friends.[3] At Camp Hollyhock, I'll get to live, eat, and mingle with girls my age every day. We'll bond while crafting, hiking, and singing. Like Mom said, my chances of successfully socializing should improve in conditions specifically engineered to promote female friendship.

My goal is to finally have made a friend by the end of the week. I just know French movie marathons, warm chocolate croissants, and slumber parties will be so much better with a companion.

Questions:

- How do I avoid the mistakes made in previous experiments?
- How do I find a friend who is the right match for me?

Future Actions:

Carefully study the girls, just like a real anthropologist, so I can better understand how to correctly approach someone with an offer of friendship.

Establish standards for evaluating whether any of my fellow campers would be appropriate candidates for potential friendship.

Endnotes:

1. Source: "Is Your Kid Ready for Camp?" April issue of *Outdoor Parenting* magazine

2. Commonly referred to as "brain freeze"

3. Source: "Girl, Get Out There!" from SparkleGirl website

Eucalyptus trees line the dirt path to the cabins. Their trunks peel as if they've been badly sunburned. I stop at a red wooden cabin framed by two skinny, flaky trees. The sign on the outside reads *Eureka*.

I hear rustling on the gravel behind me and turn to see a girl with a mane of dark, curly hair bounding up the path. She almost plows right into me. I back up to avoid physical contact and end up in a sagebrush.

"Hey, watch it!" she yells.

"Pardon me," I say as I untangle myself from the plant's purple-tipped fingers.

"Maybe if you take that lampshade off your head, you'll be able to see where you're going!" she says.

I adjust the netting that hangs from the wide brim of my straw hat. "And risk my face, neck, and head being exposed to dangerous ultraviolet radiation? No thank you."

She shrugs. "Why don't you just wear sunscreen?"

I open my mouth to inform her about the numerous cancer-causing agents found in most sunscreens, but some horrific bleating erupts from behind me. "Sofia, Fia, Fia!"

The girl—who I assume is Sofia, Fia, Fia—smiles and

runs straight toward two girls. More screaming ensues. They link arms and jump up and down until they fall over in a heap, laughing and squealing some more. This is the third such "group hug" I've seen since arriving at Camp Hollyhock.

I've never understood the appeal of a group hug. The violation of personal space, the increased risk of spreading germs, the shrieking. I shudder at the thought. However, since they seem to be common at Camp Hollyhock, I should prepare myself for the possibility of experiencing one. As an anthropologist, I must embrace every aspect of the culture I'm studying, even the ones I find unpleasant.

I swing my duffel over my shoulder and resume walking up the path, keeping my eyes peeled for a sign that reads *Clovis*. More bleating greets me, but this time, it's coming from actual goats at Camp Hollyhock's small working farm. I hold my breath to block the beastly odor and pick up my pace. In addition to the goats, the farm includes a vegetable garden, chickens, a couple of pigs, and even a cow. My stomach lurches. *E. coli, Listeria, Campylobacter.* These are the types of bacteria that run rampant in raw milk. I make a mental note to stick to water. I stop at the cabin that neighbors the farm and release my breath, thankful the sign outside the door says *Laguna*.

As I continue on, I hear chanting in the distance.

"I said a boom chicka boom! I said a boom chicka boom!"

The sounds of the chant grow louder and louder as I approach a break in the trees.

In the clearing is a small stage. Tree stumps are arranged in concentric semicircles in front of the stage to create an amphitheater. One small girl skips across the stage's gray wooden planks, bopping her head up and down.

"I said a boom chicka boom! I said a boom chicka boom!"

Campers stand on the logs, shimmying their hips and shoulders.

"I said a boom chicka rocka chicka rocka chica boom," the girl on the stage yells. Her fluffy side ponytail bounces to the beat

The girls on the logs shout back: *"I said a boom chicka rocka chicka rocka chica boom!"*

"Uh-huh," side ponytail yells.

"Uh-huh," the log chorus yells back.

"Oh yeah."

"Oh yeah."

"One more time! Valley girl style."

"Like-uh-boom chick-uh-rocka chicka gag me with a spoon!"

My head and shoulders sway to the catchy tune as I shuffle down the path. Just as they move on to surfer style,

I see a structure surrounded by a small clump of redwood trees. I veer off the path and head toward it. I stop in front of a sad, lumpy cabin, which I estimate was constructed during the late 1940s, although I can't be sure without a proper survey and test pit. A sign reading *Clovis* hangs above the door from a rusty nail. Strips of yellow paint peel off the exterior, and the front window screen is ripped.

This is it. It doesn't look like the most promising place to find a friend. Then again, penicillin was discovered in a moldy petri dish.

I pull open the screen door and step inside. The first thing I notice is a deranged dog dangling from a black backpack. Its pink matted fur springs out from its oversized plush head in pointy clumps. If it didn't have ears and whiskers, I would have mistaken it for a porcupine. Its droopy red tongue hangs below its chin, like it's dying of thirst. But the strangest thing about it? There's an odd shiny object that's sticking out from its neck.

The girl wearing the backpack swivels around. Her shiny black hair fans out and settles around a golden oval-shaped face. A name tag has been haphazardly slapped in the center of her T-shirt, right beneath her neck. The slanted letters read *Rachel Lin.* My arm jerks as my instincts tell me to fix the crooked sticker. But that would require me to violate her personal space bubble. I don't think either one of us would appreciate that.

"Oh, hi," she says. "Are you Meg?"

I point to my name tag, which clearly says *Abigail Hensley*, in straight, even letters. "No, I'm Abigail." I glance at my registration card. "It says here my roommate is Gabrielle Martin. Is she here yet?"

"Nope, we're the first ones. So I would go ahead and pick your room before anybody else gets here." She hitches her thumb at the open door behind her. "This one's mine."

Rachel twirls back around and heads into her room. The pink dog swings into the doorframe, and the silvery thing sticking out of its neck flashes as it begins to slide out. That's when I realize what the silvery thing actually is—a cell phone. As I lunge down to rescue it, my duffel throws me off balance and I tumble into Rachel.

"Seriously?" she yells, as she catches her balance on a chair and plops into its seat. "What the heck are you doing?"

I straighten into a standing position and hand her the device. "Saving your phone from a nasty fall. Nothing's worse than a splintered phone screen."

"Shhhh," she hisses. She snatches the device from my hand.

"That's probably one of the reasons why electronic devices are strictly prohibited at Camp Hollyhock," I say. "Accidental damage."

"Can you please shut it?" She wiggles out of her backpack and grabs her pink pooch.

"You mean the door? I thought you said we were the only ones here." I peek my head into the common area to double-check. The large rectangular room is empty except for a metal table and six folding chairs in the center. The sheer curtains ripple around the open picture window next to the front door. I hear a ripping noise and watch as Rachel pulls down her dog's head so its nose touches its belly.

"Is that Velcro?" I ask.

"Not that it's any of your business, but yes." She slides the phone into its belly, lifts up the dog's head, and reattaches it to the Velcro hidden inside its neck.

"That's quite a case." I say. "Did you make it yourself?"

Rachel's lips twitch at the corners, curving into a tiny smile. "Uh-huh."

"Ingenious," I say. "I wish I had thought of smuggling my phone in. It's so much easier to record my field notes on a phone than to write them by hand."

"We're not in school," Rachel says. "You won't need to take any notes."

"Since this is my first time at Camp Hollyhock, I want to record of all my experiences here," I say.

Rachel nods. "Oh, I get it. Like a diary."

I frown. "No, like field notes. Recorded in a journal."

"Whatever," she says. Rachel hugs the dog, stands up from the chair, and walks over to me. She begins to enter my personal space, so I have to take a step back. She moves closer. Again I am forced to step back. I bump into the wall.

"Relax," she says. "Dabney doesn't bite."

I laugh. "Oh, I know that. It's just that you're entering my personal space bubble."

Rachel crinkles her nose. "Your personal space bubble?"

I stretch out my arms in front of my body and make a circle. "I like to maintain a personal space buffer of three-and-a-half feet between myself and others. I'm actually quite generous with this measurement. American anthropologist Edward Hall says this bubble should reach four feet wide."

"*Okay.*" Rachel takes a step back. "Is this good?"

"Excellent."

"Anyway, I hope that Dabney here can be our little secret?" she whispers.

"Secret?" I repeat. I can't believe my luck. According to the March issue of *Tween Talk*, sharing secrets is a sign of true friendship. I wasn't expecting to make this kind of progress so early in my endeavor. "Yes, of course. Our secret. I promise I won't tell anyone." I press my pointer finger and thumb together, place them on my lips, then twist them to the left, pretending to lock my lips closed.

Rachel narrows her eyes. She seems unconvinced, so I twist my fingers back to the right, reopening my lips. "I swear. No need to worry. My mind is a vault. Figuratively speaking, of course." I point to my temple. "Obviously I don't have a safe on my head, but my brain can securely store immense amounts of information." I squeeze my eyes shut, then open them again. "There. All done. *C'est fini.*" I relock my lips.

Rachel cocks her head, studying me. "Why do you want me to say the word 'finny'?"

I reopen the lock, giggling at her charming mistake. "No, *c'est fini* is French for 'all done,' or more precisely, 'it is finished.'"

Rachel walks over to the bunk bed and places Dabney on the top mattress. "Are you, like, French?"

I sigh. "Sadly, no."

"Then what's with the outfit? You look like you just walked off the set of, like, some PBS show my mom watches."

I pull off my hat and glance down at my wide-legged culottes cinched with a chunky brown belt and topped with a khaki safari vest. "It's an appropriate outdoor outfit inspired by Jacqueline Richailbeaux, acclaimed anthropologist."

Rachel nods. "Oh yeah, that totally looks like something you would see in the window at Anthropologie." She giggles. "This Jacqueline must have some serious skills to get you to buy that."

I shake my head. "Jacqueline Richailbeaux is not a sales clerk. She is a famous character from a French movie series and the reason I aspire to be an anthropologist. She studies ancient peoples, cultures, and artifacts, and often gets swept into grand swashbuckling adventures in exotic locales."

"She sounds like a French knockoff of Indiana Jones."

I scoff. "Jacqueline Richailbeaux could eat Indiana Jones for dinner and still have room for éclairs. She's smart, fearless, and graceful—yet humble. She can do a presentation on Egyptian mummification rituals in the morning, rescue a priceless Chinese vase from filthy American pirates in the afternoon, and slip into a ball gown and dance the fox-trot at a museum fund-raiser in the evening. She is simply *magnifique.*"

"Well, whoever this chick is, your outfit is adorable."

I stiffen. Jacqueline Richailbeaux is never adorable.

The screen door squeaks.

"Why, hello, cute cozy cabin!" someone calls from the main room.

"Fia?" Rachel calls back.

"The one and only!"

Rachel makes a squeaking noise and runs out of the bedroom. "I can't believe we're in the same cabin again," she says.

"I know. So amazing, right?"

I listen to more squealing as I pick up my duffel and walk into the main room of the cabin. Rachel is embracing Sofia, Fia, Fia, the brunette girl who almost rammed into me earlier.

"Hi. We haven't been properly introduced yet," I say. "I'm Abigail."

Rachel cuts the hug short, links elbows with Sofia, and pulls her toward me.

I hold out my hand. "Nice to meet you," I say. The girls walk right past my outstretched hand and stand at the door immediately next to Rachel's chosen bedroom.

"Here, take this room, Fia," Rachel says. "That way you'll be right next door to me."

"Wait, I might have wanted that room," I say.

"Too bad. It's taken." Rachel grabs Sofia's suitcase and pushes it inside.

"But you're not following the correct room choosing protocol."

"Correct room-choosing protocol?" Sofia repeats. "Seriously?"

"Rachel was the first to arrive. She got to pick her room first," I explain. "When I arrived second, she said I could choose next."

"Yeah, but I also told you to pick before the rest showed up." Rachel shrugs. "You snooze, you lose."

"You know perfectly well I wasn't snoozing. I was saving your—"

Rachel crosses her arms and bores her brown eyes into mine.

The screen door squeaks open again. A tall, toned girl with rich brown skin walks in.

"Quinn!" Sofia and Rachel shriek. They run to greet her at the door and another group hug transpires.

After the embrace, Quinn frowns. "Why is the energy in here so toxic?"

"It's that girl's fault," Sofia says, pointing at me. "She's trying to take our room, Quinn."

"What?" Rachel throws her hands in the air. "You and Quinn are roommates? No fair!"

"Relax," Quinn says, walking the perimeter of the

common area. "At least we're all in the same cabin again." She rubs her fingers against the curtains, peers through the two doors on the other side of the room, and rolls her duffel bag around the table and chairs. "But seriously, I'm going to have to burn some calming incense in here. There are bad vibes in this place."

"Burning candles or incense is not allowed in the cabins," I say.

Quinn stops and considers me. She pulls her sunglasses down her long, slender nose.

"That's Abigail," Rachel says. "She's a stickler for protocol and personal space. So don't get any closer."

Sofia plants her hands on her hips. "She thinks because she got here second, she should get our room."

"What's the big deal?" Quinn perches her sunglasses on top of her short black pixie cut. "It's just a room."

I nod. "Good point, Quinn. It's just a room. Why can't you guys take the other one?"

"Because Fia already called dibs on this one," Rachel says through gritted teeth.

"Technically speaking, *you* called dibs for Sofia," I say. "You've already claimed your room. You shouldn't be allowed to choose two."

"Here, let's consult the Coot." Quinn pulls out a cootie

catcher from her pocket. She slips her two thumbs and pointer fingers inside some flaps in the paper.

"Should Fia and I get the room Rach chose for us?" Quinn asks. She swishes the paper around in her fingers, lifts up a flap inside, and then frowns. "'Answer unclear,'" she reads.

As Sofia and Rachel crowd around Quinn and the Coot, I take the opportunity to enter the bedroom in question.

"Hey, what are you doing?" Sofia asks.

"Sofia, call dibs," Rachel says.

Sofia runs inside the bedroom. "Dibs, dibs, dibs," she says, stomping her feet.

"Hear that?" Rachel asks as she leans against the doorjamb. "Sofia has now, technically speaking, called dibs before you." Rachel scrunches her fingers into air quotes when she says "technically speaking."

I peruse the room. It looks exactly the same as Rachel's. Beige cinder-block walls. Small desk to the left of the door. Bunk bed against the back wall. Next to the bunk is a window with another small desk directly beneath it.

"Just let the girl in the mom clothes have it already!" Quinn calls from the main room. "All this negativity is too much."

"No thank you," I say. "It's all yours."

"Un. Believe. Able," Sofia says. "After all that, you don't even want it."

"I told you," I say, walking past the girls and into the main room, "I just wanted my rightful opportunity to choose second." I cross the braided rug that covers the floor and peer through the two doors on the other side of the cabin, one of which is the bathroom. I stand in the doorway of the third bedroom. "And I choose this one."

"Too bad we can't choose another cabinmate," Sofia grumbles as she grabs Quinn's duffel bag and drags it inside the bedroom.

Quinn looks up from her paper device. "'Trouble ahead.'" She joins Sofia and Rachel inside and slams the door behind her.

I place my hat on the bottom bunk. I probably should have let the room-choosing protocol go. But if we don't have rules, we have chaos!

I pull out my field notes. I can tell I'm not off to a good start with Sofia and Quinn. But the secret phone promise allowed me to establish solid groundwork with Rachel. Because I'm keeping her confidence, she knows that I'm a true friend to her. The question now is whether she'll turn out to be a true friend to me.

Date and Time:

Sunday, June 26, 7:42 p.m.

Location:

Camp Hollyhock, Redwood Shores, California

Description of Habitat:

Camp Hollyhock is a fifty-acre campsite nestled in a forest of towering redwood trees. Our grounds include a farm, a vegetable garden, a lake, an outdoor amphitheater, a multipurpose barn where we take our meals, public restrooms that include showers, numerous hiking trails, and fifteen cabins. Each cabin houses six girls.

My cabin, Clovis, is a small wooden structure with five rooms. The squeaky front door opens into a common area that features an overhead light, a braided rug, a table, and six chairs. Three bedrooms and one small bathroom surround the common area. Each bedroom has one bunk bed, two desks, and a rug. Our bathroom consists of a toilet and sink only. Showers are housed in a separate building.

Description of Activity:

My first few hours at camp have been quite productive. After receiving cabin assignments and briefly meeting cabinmates, all campers were called to a Hollyhock Huddle at the outdoor amphitheater. There, we were introduced to the head of Hollyhock, a hulky bear of a woman who wants us to call her Hock-Eye. And, yes, she told us, it's indeed spelled *H-O-C-K*. And yes, she added, lifting her sunglasses and jutting her tanned and weathered face out, she will always have her *eye* on us.

Hock-Eye acts more like a drill sergeant than a camp director. I was expecting someone more warm and fuzzy. I do appreciate her devotion to orderliness and rules, however. She marched across the stage introducing the teen counselors who would be supervising us, commanded us to check the Chore Chart in the barn to find out our daily camp responsibilities, and then bellowed out the rules outlined in the Hollyhock Handbook. Since I had already committed this information to memory prior to my arrival, I used this time to devise a formula for measuring potential friendships. I call it the Sidekick Score.

Since Jacqueline Richailbeaux and I are both anthropologists, agile with a sword, and fluent in French, my new best friend should also resemble Jacqueline's *bonne amie* and sidekick, Mimi Le Goff. Mimi can pick locks, maneuver a Fiat down the narrowest of Paris alleyways, and make an incendiary device using only the contents of her designer handbag. Her spare and clever comments always point Jacqueline in the right direction when she's having trouble solving a puzzle. And Mimi makes delicious croque monsieurs as she listens thoughtfully (and always quietly) to Jacqueline spout off interesting archaeological trivia.

Based on this profile, the Sidekick Score will evaluate the girls according to the following character traits:

1. Adequate Street Smarts

2. Thoughtful Advising Capabilities

3. Quiet Listening Skills

The ability to make a flawless French ham-and-cheese sandwich is an added bonus, but not a requirement.

I've already started applying this matrix to some of the girls in Clovis Cabin.

Subject Rachel

Street Smarts:

Subject Rachel's ingenious apparatus for concealing her illegal electronic device should warrant a perfect 10 for Street Smarts. However, her carelessness in keeping the case tightly closed exposed her phone to a.) discovery and b.) potential destruction. I must give her a 6 out of 10 here.

Advising Capabilities:

2 out of 10. Subject Rachel thoughtlessly advised Subjects Sofia and Quinn (more on them later) to bunk in the room immediately next to hers. As an extra security measure, she should have suggested that I stay in this room. Since I was the camper who saved her phone from both discovery and potential destruction, I am the best candidate for keeping her phone protected. As demonstrated in her Street Smarts score, she could use my help in this area.

Quiet Listening:

0 out of 10. During a tour of the campgrounds earlier, Subject Rachel kept interrupting the counselors to offer unsolicited opinions and anecdotes from her previous years at Hollyhock. She giggled and whispered with Subjects Sofia and Quinn during the Hollyhock Handbook review and told Subject Sofia to "Shut up," exactly five times.

Total Score: 8 out of 30

Subject Sofia

Street Smarts:

Subject Sofia receives a 4 out of 10 here because of her fancy fingernails, which are long, pink, and sparkle with tiny jewels. Not only are they impractical, but they could also be hazardous around the campfire. Someone with adequate street smarts would know that nail polish is highly flammable. Especially someone who has been to Camp Hollyhock three years in a row.

Advising Capabilities:

I haven't heard Subject Sofia give much thoughtful advice yet. She does like to tell jokes, many of which are at others' expense. I will have to do further observations here. For now her Advising Capabilities are marked 0 out of 10.

Quiet Listening:

One would think Subject Sofia would have been offended by all the times Subject Rachel told her to shut up today, but Subject Sofia would just yell "Shut up!" right back and then laugh. In fact, Subject Sofia laughs at just about anything Subject Rachel says or does, even when Subject Rachel told us a sad story about the poor baby chick who died at Camp Hollyhock's farm last summer. Which leads to the question: Is Subject Sofia even listening to anything Subject Rachel says? Quiet Listening Score: 0 out of 10.

Total Score: 4 out of 30

Subject Quinn

Street Smarts:

Like Subjects Rachel and Sofia, Subject Quinn has also been coming to Camp Hollyhock for many years and is quite knowledgeable about the outdoors. However, her reliance on the Coot reduces Subject Quinn's Street Smarts score to a 5.

Advising Capabilities:

Subject Quinn relies on said cootie catcher for giving and receiving advice. Contrary to what its name suggests, this device does not catch cooties. Or anything, for that matter. The folded paper contraption is a prediction mechanism that I first came across when I taught myself the ancient art of origami.[1] Having learned from past mistakes,[2] I have chosen not to tell Subject Quinn it's ridiculous to believe a piece of paper can predict your future. Because of the Coot, I am forced to give her a 0 for Advising Capabilities.

Quiet Listening:

Subject Quinn doesn't talk nearly as much as the other campers. While the girls jibber-jabber away, she breathes deeply and stretches her body into all sorts of tricky yoga positions. I imagine this must take immense concentration, so I can't be sure of how much listening she's doing. However, since she is indeed the quietest girl in our cabin, I give her an 8.

Total Score: 13 out of 30

I haven't had much of a chance to observe the other two girls in Clovis Cabin. For now I will just briefly describe them.

Subject Mary Elizabeth George is Subject Rachel's roommate. She prefers to go by her initials, which spell *Meg*. Subject Meg is a tiny little thing, with dirty blond hair slicked into braided pigtails so tight, I wonder if the sides of her peachy face hurt. The rest of her is as neat and tidy as her hair, like a shiny penny. No wrinkles in her clothes, no slouching of her shoulders. She talks often about her older sister, who is a Camp Hollyhock alumna and two-time winner of the Hollyhock Honor, an award given to the most outstanding camper. When she's not speaking about her sister, she pinches her thin lips into a frown.

Subject Gabby is my roommate. She is speckled head to toe with freckles and crowned by a halo of red waves. Within moments upon entering our cabin, she gave each of us a brightly colored friendship bracelet that she made by hand. Like Subject Sofia, she is generous with her laughter, but Subject Gabby saves it for the appropriate times.

Future Action:

Our next camp activity is starting now. I will continue to observe subjects and measure friend compatibility with the Sidekick Score.

Endnotes:

1. A cootie catcher, also known as a fortune-teller, has an interior that features numerous flaps where messages have been written and concealed. Its exterior is labeled with numbers. One person chooses a number, and the other person holding the cootie catcher manipulates the device accordingly. After the final choice, the message behind the selected flap is revealed. Source: PerfectPaperProjects website.

2. See Playdate Experiment noted in previous entry.

The six inhabitants of Clovis Cabin sit cross-legged around the braided rug in the common room. Also sitting with us is our counselor, Emmy. With her slight height and fair features, Emmy doesn't actually seem that much older than us. However, what she lacks in size, she makes up for in voice. She barks out the instructions to our next camp activity, called an icebreaker. But as far as I can tell, this game has nothing to do with frozen water.

"The object of Never-Have-I-Ever is to learn something interesting about everyone here," Emmy booms. "Each of us will say something that we've never done before. I'll go first to demonstrate." She rearranges a bandana around her straw-colored hair. "Never have I ever traveled out of the country. Now, all of you who *have* traveled out of the country, raise your hands."

Three of us put our arms in the air.

"Great," Emmy says. "Now, why don't you guys say where you've been? Sofia, you first."

"Mexico," Sofia says. "We go every year to visit my abuela."

"Ooooh, I've always wanted to go there," Gabby says.

"I've been to Europe," I say.

"Oh my gosh, that sounds super fun," Gabby says.

"I went to Japan over Christmas break," Rachel says.

"Wow, that's so amazing, Rachel," Gabby says.

"Wow, that's so amazing, Rachel," Sofia says, fanning her fingers. "Brown nose much?"

Gabby laughs nervously. "What? I really do think that's amazing."

"Sofia!" Emmy barks. "Be nice. Gabby, you go next."

Gabby grabs her knees and rocks back and forth on the rug. "Hmm, let me think. Oh!" She stops rocking. "Because this is my first time at Hollyhock, never have I ever won the Hollyhock Honor."

Both Emmy and Rachel raise their hands.

"Does everyone know what the Hollyhock Honor is?" Emmy asks.

Even though we all nod, Emmy decides to tell us anyway. "You receive points throughout the week for the various activities you participate in, like placing first, second, or third in the Hollyhock Hunt, receiving medals in the Hollympics, or kissing a banana slug. Whoever gets the most points by the end of the week wins the award, which is presented on the last night of camp."

I raise my hand. "Excuse me," I say. "Are you saying that

being intimate with a slimy mollusk is a Camp Hollyhock requirement?"

"It's not required," Emmy says, "but it is a fun camp ritual. Slug smoochers receive ten extra points toward the Hollyhock Honor."

No award, not even the Nobel Prize, is worth putting my lips on a waste-eating snail. I will gladly pass on winning this achievement.

"I'm taking the Hollyhock Honor home this year," Meg says.

Emmy frowns. "The Hollyhock Honor has never been won by a first-time Hollyhocker. It's a difficult competition for newbies."

Meg crosses her arms across her chest. "Then I'll be the first first-timer to win," she says.

"I don't know about that," Sofia says, nudging Rachel. "Rachel is a tough competitor. She won it last year." Sofia points at Emmy. "She beat *you*, remember?"

"Yes," Emmy says through gritted teeth. "How could I forget?"

"You were a camper at Hollyhock last year?" I ask, now concerned about the qualifications of our rookie counselor. "How old are you?"

"Sixteen and a half," Emmy says, pulling herself taller.

"I am one of the younger counselors, but Hock-Eye says that all my years at Camp Hollyhock have given me plenty of experience to lead you girls." She claps her hands. "Now, let's get back to the game. Abigail, your turn."

I have mine ready to go. "Never have I ever traveled through time," I say.

None of my cabinmates raise their hands. They all stare at me blankly. Alas. My search for time jumpers continues.

"Okay . . . ," Emmy says. "I think it would make the game better if you gave us an activity people actually do?"

"I would argue time travel is definitely an enterprise humans can do," I say, disappointed that Emmy doesn't have a more open mind about the space-time continuum. "A hundred years ago, we didn't think space travel was possible, but clearly it is."

"That is a good point," Gabby says.

"Why thank you," I say.

Sofia sighs loudly.

"All right, then," Emmy says. She nods to the girl next to me. "Meg, why don't you go?"

Meg tilts her tiny button nose to the ceiling. "Never have I ever been sent to the principal's office."

"Ooooh, that's a juicy one," Gabby says as Quinn and Rachel raise their hands.

"Ooooh, that's a juicy one," Sofia mimics.

Sofia's Quiet Listening score would be plummeting if it wasn't already at zero.

"Sofia, cut it out," Emmy says.

Sofia rolls her eyes. "Whatever. Quinn, your turn."

Quinn puts down her cootie catcher. "Never have I ever peed in a pool." Snickers ripple around the circle of girls. I'm shocked and disgusted that mine and Meg's hands are the only ones not raised. Unfortunately, swimming with these girls will be out of the question this summer.

"Oh, I've got a good one." Sofia's brown curls shake as she bounces up and down on the carpet. "Never have I ever peed from laughing too hard." We all look at one another. Nobody raises a hand.

"But!" Sofia holds up her pointer finger. "I have made someone else pee because of a super funny story I told once."

She starts laughing, but turns it into a cough when she sees that nobody else is. Then she nudges Rachel, who sits next to her. "Yo, go," she says.

Rachel leans in to the circle. We all lean in with her. "Never have I ever kissed a boy—or a girl—on the lips."

The room falls silent. All the girls, even Emmy, whip their heads around as they look at one another.

Rachel slowly raises her hand.

"Ooooh, Rachel," Sofia says.

Wait. Why is Rachel raising her hand? Isn't she supposed to say something that she's *never* done?

I raise my own hand to ask Emmy for clarification.

"Abigail!" Rachel whistles. "You little minx."

"I'm confused," I say.

"About whether you've kissed someone?" Rachel cocks her head, and everyone giggles. "Let me give you a hint. If it happens in your dreams, it doesn't count."

The girls laugh harder now.

"That's not what I'm talking about. I mean I'm confused about the rules—"

"For kissing?" Rachel interrupts. "Well, first you have to find someone who will agree to it."

The whole room erupts in howls. Sofia is doubled over, and her brown curls tumble onto the rug. Quinn throws back her long, graceful neck and laughs at the ceiling. Meg and Gabby lean on each other, shaking with giggles. Even Emmy is smiling behind the fist she has pressed to her mouth. But it's Rachel who laughs the loudest while pointing at me.

Well, isn't that a fine thank-you-very-much. I save Rachel's phone from near destruction, and she tries to embarrass me like this? My face flushes hot with fury. She's ruining my experiment! The environment must be carefully controlled to foster potential friendships. By making me look foolish, Rachel is rendering it totally uncontrollable!

Rachel's eyes widen. She must notice my anger. "Hey, don't be like that. We're just having fun."

Emmy seems to remember she's an actual counselor and wipes the smile off her face. "Guys, that's enough. Be cool." She looks at her watch. "It's almost time for lights out, anyway." The rest of the girls rein in their laughter, and we start picking ourselves up off the floor.

Emmy clasps her hands behind her back and pushes her chest out. She reminds me of a little Chihuahua, trying to make herself look bigger around a group of Labrador retrievers. "After lights out, there is to be absolutely no activity of any kind, and that includes talking. If I were you, I'd start getting ready for bed right now, so no one's running around at the last minute trying to get their teeth brushed."

Still sitting, Rachel holds up her hand as if she wants me to help her up.

I ignore her hand.

"Seriously, Abigail, it was just a joke," she says.

"You'll get no more favors from me," I reply.

Rachel drops her hand to the ground. "Sheesh," she says. "Whatever."

Gabby pulls herself into a standing position next to me. "Sorry about all that," she whispers.

"It's okay. According to the MindScience website, it's your brain's natural impulse to mimic laughter when you encounter it." I smile at her. "I do appreciate your apology, though."

Emmy wishes us all happy Hollyhock dreams and leaves our cabin. Then we all start getting ready for bed.

After my turn in the bathroom, I walk into the room I share with Gabby, who's already tucked in bed. I flick the light switch and wait for my pupils to adjust to the darkness before I navigate to the bunk bed. Fortunately, Gabby has deemed the top bunk more desirable than the bottom. Now I'm guaranteed easy access to the exit during an emergency and reduced risk of injury from potential falls.

As the shapes in the room come into focus, I shuffle my socked feet across the warped hardwood floor and slip into bed. The bedsprings welcome me with a chorus of squeaks. I look across the room at the tiny windowpane. Another benefit to the bottom bunk: lower room temperature. Hot air always rises to the top. It will take hours for that sliver of an opening to cool this sweltering shoebox of a room. Gabby's bunk choice brings into question her Street Smarts. I must investigate further.

"Can I ask you a question?" I whisper.

"Shhhh," she whispers back. "The Hollyhock Handbook says no talking after lights out."

"True, but did you notice that it does not forbid whispering?" I ask.

"Um, I don't know, Emmy's cabin is right next door. What if she hears us?"

"First, we're separated from her bedroom by a wall, roughly fifty feet of open air, and at least two more walls," I say. "Second, according to *Outdoor Girl*, staying up late and chatting is a ritual of summer camp. As a trained counselor, I'm certain Emmy would want us to have the most authentic camp experience possible."

Gabby's mattress springs squeal as she rolls over. "Are you sure?"

"Positive." I kick the musty sheets to the bottom of the bed. "Now, my first question: What would you do if the car you were driving ran out of gas?"

Gabby doesn't answer right away. "Is this some sort of riddle?" she whispers after a moment.

"No, I'm just curious what you would do in this situation."

"But I can't drive."

I sigh. "Pretend that you can."

Gabby sighs back. "I guess I'd call my dad to come get me."

"What if your phone battery is dead? And you have to make it to a secret rendezvous with an informant? And if you don't reach him at the center of Paris's Pont Royal in exactly eighteen minutes, a precious artifact will be lost to the world forever?"

"Ooooh, Paris." The mattress springs squeak from the top bunk. "Can I be on my way to the Eiffel Tower instead?"

"The Eiffel Tower is a little obvious for a secret rendezvous, but all right." I readjust the lumpy pillow behind my head.

"If I ran out of gas in Paris," Gabby says, "I would flag down some nice French person and ask him to give me a ride to the Eiffel Tower. And then I'd tell him to step on it. You know, like they do in the movies."

I interlace my fingers and lay my hands across my stomach. "The correct answer to this conundrum is that you always keep your tank at least a quarter full, preventing the hazard of running out of gas in the first place. But yours is not a bad solution, either. I particularly liked the command 'Step on it.' '*Marche dessus*' in French." Jacqueline Richailbeaux says this often in her movies.

"Thank you, I guess," Gabby says.

A frog croaks outside our window.

"Now, what would you recommend for eliminating a nasty case of hiccups?" I ask.

"Drink a glass of water upside down," she says without hesitation.

"Pssshh." I shake my head back and forth on the pillow. "That's nonsense. It's physically impossible to drink a glass of water upside down. The water would dump out of the cup."

"But the water would pour out of the cup into your nose," Gabby says, "causing an intense case of the sneezes, which would then distract you from the hiccups, which would then go away."

I tap my pointer fingers together. "This is an interesting approach," I say. "I don't like the mess it leaves, but it is creative. Did you know that some researchers believe the hiccup is an evolutionary habit inherited from our amphibious ancestors?"

"Hmmmm?"

"Amphibious means able to live in water and on land."

"I know what it means, but—"

"Good, then you will find this theory fascinating. Before we had developed into humans, when we were once tadpole-like creatures, we gulped or hiccuped air and water through our gills. So before we had lungs, we breathed by hiccuping. That means we used to hiccup all the time. I wonder if it was as annoying then as it is now. I wonder if—"

The springs squeal again, and suddenly Gabby's face is hovering above me as she leans out of her bunk. "This authentic camp experience has been . . . interesting. But you're talking too loud, and I don't want to get in trouble. So I think we should go to sleep now." She rolls back over, and her face disappears into the darkness.

I purse my lips together. Gabby's not the quietest of listeners, but I do appreciate her willingness to follow established rules. I'll follow her advice and put myself to sleep by counting and naming all thirty-seven bridges in Paris.

Description of Activity:

We have just eaten breakfast and have returned to Clovis Cabin. My stomach gurgles and I wonder about those suspiciously runny eggs served at breakfast this morning. I hope they were cooked thoroughly. The subjects are chatting while packing backpacks for a hike down to the lake. Actually, a more accurate description is yelling. They shout insults at one another like "Shut up," "Get out," and "You're such an idiot." The subjects on the receiving end of this disparagement don't seem the least bit bothered. Most of the time, they just explode in equally loud laughter.

My roommate, Subject Gabby, deviates from this behavior and lavishes everyone with compliments instead: "Rachel, your hair is *soooo* long and pretty. Quinn, that cootie catcher is awesome. Would you make one for me?"

I find myself smiling warmly at Subject Gabby, but interestingly, none of the other subjects respond positively to this flattery. In fact, Subjects Sofia and Rachel often roll their eyes at her. You don't have to be an anthropologist to know that the eye roll is a young girl's universal signal of annoyance.

Reflections:

As I watch the subjects delight in being teased and taunted, I recall how Subject Rachel treated me during the icebreaker last night. She teased and ridiculed me too. In light of what I'm observing now, an interesting question emerges. Was Subject Rachel expressing her appreciation for my help in saving her phone and keeping her secret by making fun of me? And are she and Subject Sofia trying to signal to Subject Gabby that they prefer to be insulted, not complimented?

Flattering someone by insulting them is certainly the reverse approach to making human connections. But perhaps rude and disagreeable behavior is more attractive to these girls than kindness. This reminds me of that time when I was still in middle school, and the so-called "popular" girls spent an entire day being kind to me. When I asked what brought about the sudden change in behavior, I was informed that it was Opposite Day.[1] Indeed, the very next day, they went back to calling me Scabby Abby and tripping me at lunchtime. I'm so glad those dismal days are long gone. Though I don't have any friends in high school, nobody is going out of their way to make me miserable.

Could these subjects be applying this Opposite Day phenomenon to their friendships? I must keep this behavior in mind as I continue with my observations. Speaking of which, I have evaluated Subject Gabby's Sidekick Score.

Her solution to the empty gas tank conundrum wasn't the one I would have chosen, but it was definitely inspired. I give her a 6 out of 10 for Street Smarts. Her advice on halting hiccups was also helpful, so she receives an 8 out of 10 for Advising Capabilities. Though she didn't seem that interested in my thoughts on early amphibious breathing, she does seem to value silence. Therefore, I'm awarding her a 7 for Quiet Listening. So far, she has the highest score of 21 out of 30. A very promising start.

However, numbers are only part of the equation. Do I actually like my roommate? I consider her pleasantness, her thoughtful answers to my questions, and her interest in French culture. My answer is yes! This experiment is off to a fabulous start. How exciting that Subject Gabby might end up being my new best friend! Her name even has French origins! Though why she has chosen to shorten the beautiful Gabrielle to an unimaginative nickname is beyond me. When our friendship is solidified, I will persuade her to reconsider.

Endnote:

1. An event that occurs annually on January 25, according to the National Observances website

I hug my flaming abdomen. It's like fireworks are exploding inside. Those cursed eggs! I knew they were going to be trouble. I should have chosen cereal, like the rest of Clovis Cabin. Undercooked yolks are a breeding ground for salmonella enteritidis bacteria, which often leads to gastrointestinal illness. That must be why I'm camped out here in the bathroom instead of at the lake with the rest of the girls.

Somebody pounds on the door, scaring me halfway to Hades. I didn't think anyone was left in the cabin.

"Hurry up in there!" It's Sofia. "I gotta go!"

I spew more stomach bile into the toilet bowl.

"Never mind," she calls from behind the door. "I guess I'll hold it. Catch ya later, Hurl Girl!" She cackles as she leaves the cabin, slamming the front door behind her.

According to the March issue of *Glossy Girl*, receiving a fun nickname is supposed to be an honor, symbolizing you've been accepted among your peers. However, I'm not feeling terribly honored at this moment.

I flush and turn on the faucet to splash my face with

cold water. Then I stumble into my bedroom and curl up on the thin mattress of my bottom bunk.

My mind flips through a slideshow of nausea remedies I once saw on a medical website. *Try ginger. This miracle root causes your body to secrete digestive juices to fight angry stomach acids.*

I suddenly miss Dad and the ginger candies that he always carries around in his pocket. No ginger here at Camp Hollyhock. Hock-Eye had only antacids in her medical kit.

My stomach lurches again. Just as I'm about to make another trip to the bathroom, I hear the cabin door quietly open and close. *Not Sofia again,* I think. I breathe deeply, counting her steps, hoping the mental focus will distract my revolting stomach.

After exactly seven steps, Sofia leaves the cabin without bothering me. The front door thunks shut, followed by the squeal of the screen door closing. I jump out of bed, run to the bathroom, and make it to the toilet just in time. After another round of retching, I pour myself a glass of water, sip it slowly, and return to bed.

I recall more advice from the medical website. *Acupressure can neutralize vomiting. Press down on the two tendons inside your wrist.*

This I can do. I push down my right thumb on the

underside of my left wrist. The swirling in my stomach slows.

The wind picks up outside. The screen door bangs. Tree branches scrape against the window. I close my eyes and listen as the air whips through the cabin's outdoor siding.

The next time I open my eyes, it's dark. I must have slept through the day. The light from the common area pours into my bedroom. Quinn stands in the doorway, holding a tray with a bowl.

"Hey," she says. "Want some soup?"

I pull myself out of the bunk and take the food. "Thank you." I'm flattered Quinn has taken a liking to me. "That's so thoughtful."

"Whatever." She lifts her leg and presses it against her ear in one of her yoga poses.

Sofia said the exact same thing to Gabby last night. Quinn must not like my compliment. Now's the perfect time for an Opposite Day experiment. I'll insult her and see what happens.

"Okay . . . well . . . get out!" I say.

Quinn drops her pose. "Your energy needs work. Too negative." As she leaves my room, she turns and calls over her shoulder. "If you're done puking, we're roasting marshmallows by the campfire."

An invitation to a time-honored camp bonding experience? My insult worked!

"Let me see if I can get this down first," I say.

Quinn shrugs and floats out the bedroom doorway.

I take the tray over to the small desk in the corner, grab the bowl, and sniff. The smell doesn't trigger any stomach activity. I sip carefully and wait. I try another sip. The broth is watery and too salty, but I'm famished, so I drink it down.

Something crashes in the main room, and Quinn moans.

"You okay?" I call out.

The cabin goes silent. "Uh-huh," she says.

"Did you know that ten percent of yoga injuries require a visit to the hospital?" I ask.

"Uh-huh."

"So be careful in those poses. I would hate for you to end up in the hospital. Those places are crawling with germs!"

Quinn responds by slamming the cabin door. Interesting. She reacts to my concern about her well-being by ignoring me and storming out. More evidence for my Opposite Day Behavior, or ODB, theories.

I debate joining the girls for roasted marshmallows. On the one hand, it sounds like a great opportunity for bonding, but on the other, eating food off a stick isn't sanitary. My body has fought enough bacteria today. When everyone returns, I'll suggest a pillow fight. According to the TweenScene website, they're supposed to be popular at slumber parties and apparently generate lots of squeals and giggles. Perhaps I'll try squealing and giggling myself. I stand in front of the bathroom mirror and practice a few shrieks. I decide a simple toothy grin will work better.

With that settled, I wiggle into my PJs printed with tiny images of Paris monuments and climb into bed with the mystery novel I brought, *Murder on the Orient Express*. Just as the doomed train screeches to a halt in a giant snowbank, the door to Clovis Cabin bursts open. Someone's singing. *"I said a dude chicka dude."* It sounds like Meg.

I drop the book, grab a pillow, and head out of my bedroom.

"I said a dude chicka wipe out chicka whoa chicka dude." Meg's singing in the bathroom.

The main room is empty. A chair is turned on its side. I set it back upright as I wait for Meg to come out, holding my pillow aloft. She opens the door. I smack her on the arm with my pillow. Her flashlight drops and rolls across the floor.

She does not squeal or giggle. Instead she pinches her tiny thin lips together. "Seriously?" she finally says. "What was that for?"

I smash the pillow on her head. "I'm engaging you in a pillow fight."

"Stop it," she says, ducking away from my next blow. "Pillow fights are dangerous."

"They are?" I ask. "I thought pillow fights were common at camp."

"My sister says they can cause serious injury," Meg says. "Now what happened to my flashlight?"

We hunt around the floor. I point toward a beam of light shining from Meg's room. "It must have rolled in there," I say.

She sighs like she has to hike through the Sierra Nevada mountains to go fetch the flashlight.

After Meg enters the darkened room, she shrieks. She dashes back into the main room, grabs my shoulders, and shakes me so hard I drop my pillow. "Someone's in there," she says. "I saw a face. Whoever it is, they're still inside."

I shake my head. "There's no one else here but me. You must have seen a shadow."

"Nope." Meg shakes her head wildly. "I saw a face. I know it."

I disentangle myself from her clutches, pick up my pillow, and walk toward the room.

"What are you doing?" she asks.

"Proving there's no one in there."

Meg grabs me again. "Are you nuts? My sister says crazy ax murderers live out in the wilderness. One must have snuck in here." She runs toward the front door. "I'm getting Hock-Eye."

As Meg runs back out into the night, I walk into her room and flick on the light. Just as I'm bending to pick up Meg's flashlight, something moves in my peripheral vision. I swallow and turn to look. It's a face. I take a deep breath as I recognize it. It's my face. Reflecting in a mirror on the desk. I shake my head.

"Meg!" I call. "I told you there's nobody in there. You just saw your—"

"What the heck are you doing in here?" someone interrupts.

I spin around. Rachel stands at the door, her hands on her hips and her eyes narrowed.

"Nothing," I say. "Your roommate got scared. She thought there was an ax murderer hiding in here. But as you can see, there's not."

I place Meg's flashlight on the desk next to the mirror. I walk back to my own room while Rachel starts to climb onto her bunk bed. As I'm returning the pillow to my bunk, Rachel shouts an obscenity.

I peek into the common area to see what's causing the alarm. Rachel's coming right at me, shaking a pink fluffy ball in her hand. "I know what you were really doing in my room," she yells. "Now give it back!"

I step back and extend my arms to stop her from getting too close. She thrusts Dabney in my face. The crazed little dog looks even weirder than normal. It seems to be missing its entire body below the neck.

"What happened to Dabney?" I ask.

Rachel rolls her eyes dramatically. "Don't act like you don't know." She holds up her other hand, holding the remains of the wretched dog.

"But I *don't* know."

Voices outside the cabin interrupt us. Sofia throws open the screen door and jumps into the common area. She plants herself with legs apart and pushes up the short sleeves of her T-shirt. "Hiii–yah!" she yells, waving her arms around. "Hear that, creepo? That's the sound of a brown belt in karate."

"False alarm," I say. "There're no creepos in here."

"Except for you, Abigail." Rachel glares at me.

"But what about that face I saw?" Meg tiptoes inside. Gabby follows behind her.

"It was your reflection in the mirror," I say.

"Now I get why she was so spooked," Sofia says as she breaks out of her karate stance. "Her face scares me too."

Meg's heart-shaped face is actually quite harmless. Her big brown eyes are almost perfectly aligned on either side of her button nose. Studies show that such facial symmetry demonstrates scientific proof of attractiveness.

Interesting. Meg doesn't laugh like the girls normally do when they're flattered by insults. She must not recognize Opposite Day Behavior.

"Ugly jokes, really?" Meg asks. "*Real* mature."

Should I tell Meg about my findings about ODB? Or keep quiet and risk her social standing in order to study how her behavior affects the group? Oh, the ethical dilemmas of an anthropologist!

"'Trouble ahead,'" Quinn says, reading from her cootie catcher as she closes the heavy wooden door behind her.

"That's right. *Lots* of trouble ahead." Rachel stands in the center of the room, shaking the stuffed dog head in the air. "Look what Abigail did. Look what she did to my Dabney!"

Some of the girls gasp, sucking in so much air I swear I feel my ponytail move. Quinn and Sofia huddle around Rachel. After hugging one another and clucking over the destroyed dog, they all turn to glare at me.

"I'm afraid Rachel is mistaken," I say. "I haven't touched Dabney."

"What's the big deal, anyway?" Meg asks. "It's just a stuffed animal."

"Dabney is not *just* a stuffed animal," Rachel says. "I've slept with him every night since I was five years old. I love this dog and she, like, murdered it!"

"Excuse me, but I must clarify something," I say. "You can't murder something that was never technically alive to begin with. I would describe poor Dabney here as desecrated or vandalized, but certainly not—"

"Stop distracting us with the fancy words," Rachel says, holding out her hand. "Just hand over my phone."

Gabby cocks her head. "What phone?" she asks.

"I don't have your phone," I say. "Are you saying it's missing?"

"Hold on!" Meg plants her tiny hands on her tiny hips. "Phones aren't allowed at camp."

Rachel folds her arms across her chest. "What are you gonna do? Tell on me?"

"According to the Hollyhock Handbook, I should."

The girls start murmuring among themselves.

Meg raises her voice. "If I don't report someone who I know is breaking camp rules, I can be punished too. My sister told me so. And she should know. She went to camp here for, like, seven years." Meg sweeps her arm around the room. "Right now, all of us are breaking camp rules by not reporting Rachel."

Meg and her sister are indeed correct. The Hollyhock Handbook specifically says it is our duty to report girls who break camp rules. This is another interesting ethical dilemma. Will the girls risk their own standing at camp to protect Rachel? And more importantly, will Rachel gamble with putting herself in trouble to tell Hock-Eye a falsehood—that I took her illegal device?

"We could *all* get in trouble?" Gabby asks as her gaze darts around the room.

"Relax," Rachel says. "It's just a phone, not a bag of drugs."

Sofia pops her head out of the bathroom. "Drugs? Who's got drugs?"

Quinn looks up from her cootie catcher. "'Ask again later.'"

Sofia storms into the main room. "If I get caught with some loser packing drugs, I'm off the soccer team."

"My sister says last year, Alexa Feingold got kicked out of camp when—"

"Oh, that's totally not why she got—"

"'Outlook not so good.'"

The girls shout and yell over one another. My eyes bounce from girl to girl like a Ping-Pong ball as I try to focus on who is saying what until a piercing whistle rips through the room, silencing everyone. We all look toward the noise.

Rachel takes her thumb and pointer finger out of her mouth. "Okay. First thing, no one's got any drugs."

"They better not," Sofia says.

"And the more important thing is that Abigail took and broke my private property," Rachel says. "That's gotta be a way worse offense than me forgetting to leave my phone at home."

All eyes are on me again. A flash of heat surges down my spine, and I squeeze my hands into tight fists. I can't allow for untruths to be spread about me, especially when they threaten my future here at camp. Thievery is grounds for automatic dismissal, according to the Hollyhock Handbook. I cannot get sent home. Not when my experiment is going so well.

"I did not steal your phone," I say through clenched teeth, "which, by the by, you purposely smuggled to camp inside Dabney. Why do you keep accusing me?"

"Three reasons." Rachel holds up one finger. "You're the only one who knew about it." She holds up another finger.

"You've been here all day by yourself." She holds up a third finger. "And I just caught you sneaking around in my room."

"I already told you. I was checking to make sure no one was in there."

"Shhhh," Gabby says. "Did you hear that?"

We fall silent and look around the room at one another, straining our ears.

Sofia shakes her head. "I don't hear—"

Gabby waves her hands. "Shhhhhhh. There it is again."

"She's right," Meg says. "I hear it too. It's coming from in there." She points toward the bedroom that she and Rachel share. We all turn to look.

Something thumps inside.

Sofia screams. It's one of those brittle screeches that scrapes your throat just as hard as it pierces the air.

"What?" Sofia says as we all look at her. "I got spooked."

"I told you," Meg whispers. "Someone's in there. I'm never wrong."

I recall the inside of the room with the smudged white walls and brown wood-planked floors. I remember the duffel bags tucked underneath the bottom bunk, the mirror on the desk, and the small window to the side of the beds. Of course. The window.

I march toward the bedroom.

Quinn waves her cootie catcher in the air. "'Trouble ahead.'"

Gabby grabs my arm. "Are you sure you want to go in there?"

I shake my arm free from her grasp. "Positive."

As I cross the doorway, something in the room thumps again. A couple of girls squeal.

"Inhale, exhale, inhale, exhale," Quinn chants.

"We're all going to die," Meg says.

"We are not going to die," I say, heading toward the window. I pull up the dusty plastic blinds. "Come and look. It's just the wind knocking the window shades."

The girls huddle around the doorway. "See." I give the blinds a little push and they bump against the window frame.

All five girls release one long sigh.

The blinds twist in the wind. As they knock against the frame again, I see something missing. I look behind the blinds. "Did you guys notice there was no screen here?"

Meg joins me at the window. "I didn't even realize it was open," she says. She looks at Rachel. "Did you open it?"

Rachel shakes her head.

"Hmm . . . maybe you were right, Meg," I say. "Maybe someone was in here, after all." I study the little square window. It's about five feet from the floor. I poke my head through. "It would be a tough climb and a tight fit, but possible," I say.

"You're just saying that to keep the blame off you," Rachel says.

I ignore her. "The criminal would have had to jump down from this height. Probably landing here." I stand about a foot away from the window and study the floor. Something sparkles nearby. I squat to get a closer look. It's a tiny pink crystal. I pick it up and show it to Sofia. "Does this belong to you?"

Sofia looks at her hands. The flowers etched on her hot-pink painted fingernails feature a jeweled center. All except one.

"Oh," she says quietly. "Thanks." She slips it into her pocket.

I return to inspecting the immediate surroundings. Underneath the ladder to the top bunk is a blue plaid water bottle. I bend to pick it up. *MEG* is monogrammed on the side.

"This must be yours," I say.

Meg grabs the bottle out of my hand, her eyes wide. She blinks at me. "Yes, it's totally mine," she says, after a moment's thought. "But so what? This is my room too."

She grabs the ladder attached to the bunk bed, swings around it, and plops onto the bottom bunk. A figure made out of paper bounces off the comforter and onto the floor.

Gabby picks it up, turns it around in her fingers, and hands it to Quinn. "This cootie catcher yours?"

Quinn grabs it. A little too quickly. She shrugs. "Signs point to maybe."

Someone knocks at the front door. "Girls, it's me."

"It's Emmy," Sofia whispers. "What are you going to do about your phone, Rachel?"

"If you tell her Abigail stole it, you'll have to admit you broke camp rules," Quinn whispers. "Outlook not good."

"And if we don't tell her, we'll all be breaking the rules," Meg says.

"More importantly, you'd all be lying," I add. "I didn't steal the phone."

The screen door squeals. "You guys good in here?" Emmy asks.

"Yes!" Rachel yells.

"No!" Meg yells at the exact same time.

Rachel glares at Meg. "Not a word about the . . . ," Rachel mimes the phone signal with her hand and holds it up to her ear. "Okay?"

"No, it's not okay. It's wrong," Meg whispers. She heads toward the doorway.

Rachel grabs her arm. "Please. I'll owe you big time."

Meg shakes off Rachel's grip and heads out of the bedroom. We all follow Meg into the common area.

"There you are," Emmy says. "I heard someone scream. Everything okay?"

Meg opens her mouth, but Rachel beats her to it.

"Someone murdered my dog, Dabney!" she yells before throwing herself onto Emmy and grabbing her in a hug. Our little counselor almost disappears into Rachel's embrace.

That's curious. Rachel didn't accuse me in front of Emmy. Does this mean she's come to her senses?

"That's horrible!" Emmy says, hugging Rachel back.

Rachel continues hugging Emmy, slowly turning her around so Emmy faces away from us. She looks over Emmy's head and eyes Meg. She mouths the word *please*.

Emmy pulls herself away from Rachel. "I'm so sorry," she says. "But I'm a little confused. How did you find out about your dead pet between the campfire and now?"

Rachel wipes beneath her eyes. "Oh, I don't have a real dog." She hands Emmy the severed head. "This is Dabney."

Emmy turns the pink ball of fluff over in her hands. "Where's the rest of him?"

Rachel shows her Dabney's headless body.

"So you're telling me someone ripped the head off your stuffed dog?" Emmy asks.

Rachel nods.

Emmy tugs at one of her braided pigtails. "Why would someone do something like that?"

Rachel stares right at me. "Because they're a freak, I guess."

Emmy points the head at us. "Do any of you know what happened to Dabney?"

I shake my head and look at the other girls. Quinn, Gabby, and Sofia also shake their heads.

Meg nods hers up and down. "Well . . . ," she says.

We all look at her. Rachel drops into a chair and closes her eyes.

Emmy gingerly places Dabney's severed head onto the table. "Yes, Meg?"

"Someone might have broken into the cabin," she answers. "Our window was open. And I thought I saw someone in my room earlier."

I raise my hand. "If I may interrupt. I hypothesize that Meg mistook her reflection in a mirror for a prowler. But she is correct in suggesting that someone could have squeezed through that window sometime today."

Emmy clasps her hands behind her back. "Was anything taken?"

"No," Rachel stands up from her chair. "Nothing else."

"I should tell Hock-Eye about this." Emmy walks into Meg and Rachel's bedroom. "I'm just going to take a look around and make sure everything else checks out, okay?"

"Okay," we all murmur.

After Emmy leaves the common area, Rachel hugs Meg tightly. "Thank you, thank you, thank you," she whispers.

Meg pulls Rachel's arms off her. "Like you said," she whispers, "you owe me. Big time. So tomorrow you're going to be my partner in the Hollyhock Hunt."

"But Rach and I are always partners," Sofia whines. "We win every year!"

"I know," Meg says. "That's why I want to partner with her."

"How about instead of the scavenger hunt, I do your daily Hollyhock chore, instead?" Rachel asks.

Meg shrugs. "Okay, then. I'll just let Emmy know what was hiding inside Dabney." She heads toward her bedroom doorway.

Rachel jogs over to block Meg's way. "No, it's fine. I can be your partner tomorrow."

Sofia groans.

"Sorry, Fia," Rachel says.

Emmy emerges from the bedroom and proceeds to look in all our rooms. Even the bathroom. "Well, everything else checks out. Nobody's hiding under the bunks or behind doors. If you notice anything else damaged or missing, let me know."

"We will," Rachel says.

"Lights out is in fifteen minutes," Emmy says, puffing up again. "Remember, no talking or fooling around. Hock-Eye caught Laguna Cabin last night playing light-as-a-feather-stiff-as-a-board, and instead of hiking today, they all had to clean the chicken coop."

A gag reflex causes my body to heave violently at such a horrific task.

"And they each got a strike," Emmy continues. "You remember what happens after three strikes, right?"

"You're outta here!" Sofia throws her arm up and back like an umpire.

Emmy smiles and heads toward the front door. "Night, girlies! Happy Hollyhock dreams!"

The door closes. "How are we supposed to have Happy Hollyhock dreams when there's a thief running around?" Meg asks.

"Luckily, our thief is right here in this cabin, so we can all keep an eye on her," Rachel says, glaring at me.

"What?" I ask. "You still think I did it? I thought you'd moved on from that nonsense."

Rachel shakes her head. "I am not a snitch. But I know you stole my phone. If you don't return it soon, I'm definitely telling Hock-Eye, and you'll be out of here. I'll make sure of it."

Before I can object, she swings around and stomps into the bathroom. Quinn, Sofia, and Meg head to their bedrooms.

Gabby beckons me to come close to her. I obey but stop short of piercing her three-and-a-half-foot personal space bubble. "Quick," she whispers. "While she's in the bathroom, try to slip the phone inside her pillowcase or something."

I suck in a breath. Gabby actually believes I committed this crime?

"Maybe you can convince her she misplaced it," Gabby continues, before walking into our own room.

I open my mouth to reply, but I am stunned speechless. I drop into a chair, feeling ill again. But this time, my nausea has nothing to do with pesky bacteria. I am sick that my own roommate believes Rachel over me. This could have disastrous effects on my experiment.

From the table, I watch my cabinmates shuffle from bathroom to bedroom and back again, talking, giggling, and insulting one another. They don't give me a second look, or even a first look, for that matter. I clench my fists, frustrated at another experiment gone awry. The results were supposed to be different this time. But yet again, I'm floating around the periphery of this group of girls, like a forgotten balloon bobbing around the ceiling.

Date and Time:

Monday, June 27, 9:56 p.m.

Location:

Camp Hollyhock, Redwood Shores, California

Description of Activity:

Subject Rachel has falsely accused me of "murder." Despite my denials, my cabinmates believe her and not me. I am doing my best to evaluate this unfortunate turn of events from a scientific point of view.

Reflections:

My hypothesis for the girls' behavior is *herd mentality*, when people or animals do what others around them do to fit in with the larger group.[1] A recent poll conducted on the popular website TweenScene supports my theory. It listed "fitting in with friends" as the number-one concern for twelve-year-old girls.[2]

As herd mentality seems to be a reaction the girls cannot control, I am trying not to take their slights personally. However, I must be honest. My feelings are hurt. Scientifically speaking, these feelings are probably another natural response beyond my self-control. Personally speaking, I want to abandon science for a few brief moments and wallow in my misery. But I don't have time for such nonsense.

Subject Rachel's accusations are already negatively affecting my experiment. Preliminary results were pointing to Subject Gabby as the best choice for potential friendship. Not only does she have the highest Sidekick Score (21 out of 30), I also actually like her. Alas, she too has fallen for Subject Rachel's falsehoods. She might not want to be best friends with an alleged thief, vandalizer, or liar. I know that I would not want such a friend.

I must prove to Subject Gabby and the rest of these girls I'm innocent and get my experiment back on track. Otherwise, failure is certain. And where exactly do I go from here? Past experiments have shown that I can't make friends at school or in clubs of any kind. What does it say about me that I can't make friends at camp, which, as previously cited in these field notes, is the ideal place to make lifelong friends? Troubling questions like these are why I must put off diving into my emotions and stay focused on solving the problem at hand.

Questions:

- Who did, in fact, commit the crime that Subject Rachel is so upset about? Is that person in our cabin?

Future Action:

Discover who the real thief is to clear my name.

Endnotes:

1. Source: October issue of *Young Anthropologist*

2. Source: "Tween Stressors," TweenScene website

The bedsprings squeak beneath me as I roll onto my side and look out the window. An almost-full moon peeks through the trees. As the wind rustles the leaves, light dances across the floor. A small breeze teases our stuffy sauna of a room. Even the frogs agree it's too hot to sleep. They squabble at one another in frenzied bursts of croaking.

"Are you awake?" Gabby whispers.

"Yes."

Gabby leans her head over the side of her bed. Her red hair shimmers in the moonlight. "Why did you rip up Dabney and steal Rachel's phone?"

I sit straight up and scrape my head on the steel coils above me. "Oww." I rub my head but only succeed in getting more hair tangled in the bed above me.

"Shhhh," Gabby hisses. She climbs down from her bunk and curls up on the end of my mattress. She's closing in on my perimeter of personal space.

"Were you trying to get back at her because she made fun of you during the icebreaker?" she asks.

I pull at the strands of my hair. "How many times

do I have to explain myself? I didn't decapitate Rachel's dog or steal her phone. I pinky swear." *All-American Girl Magazine* says the pinky swear is the most sacred of all swears.

"Then who do you think did?" Gabby reaches over to untangle my hair, definitely breaching my bubble's barrier. I try to pull away, but the mattress springs above have a tight hold on my hair. I wince at my stinging scalp.

"Stay still," Gabby says, tugging at my head.

Someone taps at the door. "Everyone okay?" The door opens a crack, and Meg pokes her head in. "I heard someone yell."

"Abigail hit her head."

"Uh-oh." Meg turns on her flashlight and shines it in our direction. "My sister says you should be careful with a head injury."

"She's fine," Gabby says.

The bedsprings cry as Meg climbs onto the bed. She aims her beam right into my face. I have to squeeze my eyes shut to avoid the harsh light.

"Looks like your pupils aren't dilated," she says. "That's a good sign. Do you know what day it is?"

"Monday around ten p.m. I didn't hit my head *that* hard."

"Can you please stop squirming?" Gabby asks. "And Meg, please aim your flashlight up a little."

I wince as Gabby tugs at my hair and breathes on my forehead. I also breathe deeply to assure myself that the discomfort I'm feeling from the personal space invasion might be beneficial in this instance. I'm encouraged that both girls are taking an interest in my well-being. Perhaps they haven't been fooled by Rachel's false accusations after all.

"Have you received first-aid training, Meg?" I ask.

"Not really," she says. "But I know how to do a concussion check and treat a sprained muscle. Most people think just ice and elevation. But alternating heat with the ice every few minutes helps circulation and healing."

"That is excellent advice," I say.

She shrugs. "That's what my sister says, anyway."

Too bad Meg's sister isn't part of my experiment. From what Meg tells me, she would have high marks in the Sidekick Score.

"Your sister," I say. "What's her name?"

"Madeline Elise George," Meg says.

"Oh cute," Gabby says. "You guys have the same initials."

"Nothing about Madeline is cute," Meg says.

"Yeah, she sounds like a know-it-all," Gabby says, still working hard on my tangled hair. "If she were my sister, she would so get on my nerves."

"She would?" I ask, surprised by Gabby's answer for two reasons. First, this is the first time I've ever heard her utter a disparaging comment. Second, I can't understand why someone would be irritated to receive information from a knowledgeable peer.

Meg giggles. "Actually, she does get to me sometimes. Just because I use a different method for multiplying two digits doesn't mean I'm doing it wrong. But I can't tell her that."

"I'd like to clarify something, if I may," I say. "Are you saying you don't like receiving sound advice from an experienced peer?"

Gabby shakes her head. "Most know-it-alls are just show-offs."

I feel the last strands of hair pull away from the coils. "There," Gabby says. "Got it."

Free at last. I inch up the bed, pressing myself against the headboard, and hug my knees close to my chest. "Thank you," I say to Gabby. "And thank you both for that interesting insight."

"What are you guys doing in here?" Sofia asks, tiptoeing

into the room. Quinn follows behind her. "Keeping watch over the thief?"

"She swears she didn't steal Rachel's phone," Gabby says. "I believe her, and you guys should too."

I smile at Gabby. Excellent advice. Her Sidekick Score is rising.

"Of course you believe her, Gabby. You think everyone is just so amazing!" Sofia sprawls out on our room's Southwestern-style rug. "If it wasn't Abigail, then who?" she asks.

"'Reply hazy.'" Quinn fiddles with her cootie catcher. "'Ask again later.'" She slides into a split on the floor.

"The Coot actually has a point," I say. "The answer is hazy because any of you could have stolen Rachel's phone."

The girls start buzzing like a swarm of African killer bees.

"Uh, I know you just didn't go and accuse me," Sofia says, pointing one of her long pink talons at herself.

I trudge ahead. "You were in the cabin for a few moments after the rest of the girls left for the lake," I say. "You would have had plenty of time to steal the phone."

"Abigail's right," Meg says, snapping her fingers. "We got a late start because we were waiting on you."

"Not because I was stealing a phone," Sofia says.

"And what about that nail jewelry of yours?" Gabby asks. "Abigail found it on the floor next to the beds."

"So what?" Sofia says. "Quinn's cootie catcher was found there too. And so was Meg's water bottle."

"You're all proving my point," I say. "The evidence points to multiple persons of interest."

The girls drone, louder this time.

"I just got a bad nail job, that's all."

"Maybe someone else did it. Don't forget, Meg swears someone was in her room."

"Answer unclear."

"Shhhh," someone hisses from the doorway. Meg aims her beam at the noise.

Rachel holds up a hand to shield her eyes from the light. She steps inside, closing the door. "Give it up, Abigail," Rachel says. "You stole my phone. Stop trying to pretend you didn't and give it back."

"I am not pretending. And just because you think I broke it doesn't make it true. There's plenty of evidence pointing to other people in this cabin. Even you."

The girls gasp.

"Me?" Rachel squeaks. "Don't be dumb. Why would I steal my own phone?"

"Maybe you lost it by accident, and you need to blame

someone else to get a new one. So you're framing me," I say.

Even in the darkness, I can see a flicker of rage in Rachel's eyes. She lunges toward me. Quinn leaps up from her split and grabs her before she can get to me. "Whoa," she says. "Violence is not the answer."

Rachel reaches around Quinn and points at me. "You're gonna get it."

Gabby clears her throat. "Rachel, why are you so sure Abigail stole your phone, anyway?"

Rachel shrugs Quinn away from her. "She told me yesterday how she wished she had brought her own phone. How she needed it to record notes or whatever. Maybe she thought she could take mine for herself."

"Signs point to maybe," Quinn says.

"This is ridiculous," I say. "Do you people know anything about innocent until proven guilty?"

"Of course we do," Rachel says. "We did a mock trial in social studies last year."

"Hey, let's do another one," Sofia says. "Right now, so we can figure out if Abigail really stole the phone."

Meg bounds over to the corner desk and sits in the chair. "I call being judge," she announces.

"No fair!" Sofia points at Meg. "How come you get to be judge?"

Meg clasps her hands and places them on the desk. "Because I called it first."

Sofia opens her mouth to object, but realizing she can't argue with first dibs, snaps it closed in a pout.

"I call bailiff," Quinn says. She stands by the closed door.

"This all sounds super fun," Gabby says as she weaves her red hair through her fingers, "but maybe we should do this tomorrow. We can't let Hock-Eye catch us talking past lights out. We don't want to miss the scavenger hunt tomorrow."

"Oh yeah," Meg says. "I need to win to get points for the Hollyhock Honor."

"This is pointless anyway," Rachel says. "We already know who's guilty."

"But she wasn't given a fair trial," Sofia says. "Everyone deserves their day in court."

"That is true," Meg says. "My sister says that the one time a year she gets in trouble." She pulls on one of her braided pigtails. "Do you guys promise to keep your voices quiet?"

The other girls nod.

Rachel groans. "Fine. I'll play along, just so we can close this case for good." She pulls the chair out from the other desk and places it in the center of the rug. "Meg, as the judge, you're in charge of the flashlight. Keep it low. Since it's my phone, I'll be a lawyer, the persecuting one."

"You mean the 'prosecuting' attorney," I say.

"Whatever," Rachel says. "Who wants to be the other lawyer, the one who handles Abigail?"

Gabby raises her hand and wiggles around on the mattress like a kindergartner whose bladder is about to burst.

"Fine, you represent her," Rachel says.

Gabby scrambles out of bed and stands proudly next to Rachel.

The night's events have completely taken me by surprise. Just a few hours earlier I thought we'd be throwing pillows at one another willy-nilly. The girls are doing something I find mildly interesting— even if I am the one who's on trial.

"If it pleases the court," I say, "I'd like to represent myself."

"It doesn't *please* the court," Rachel says. "Gabby's your lawyer. Deal with it."

I sigh. "It's not up to you," I say. "The judge has the final say on whether a defendant can defend herself." Clearly Rachel has forgotten the lessons from her trial unit. I walk over to Meg. "Your Honor, may I please represent myself?"

Meg scratches her temple as if she's actually deliberating and then nods. "I'll allow it."

"But now *I* have nothing to do," Gabby whines.

"You can be our first witness," I offer.

"No, I want Fia," Rachel says.

Sofia jumps up from the rug. She grabs the other desk chair, sets it next to Meg's corner desk, and perches on the edge of it. Quinn stands guard at the door. Gabby flounces back to the edge of my bed and sulks.

Rachel stands on the rug between the bunks and the "bench" of our mock courtroom. She rolls back her shoulders to stand as straight and tall as she can. "Sofia, what was the murderer doing when you saw her this morning before the hike?"

I stand up from the bottom bunk. "Objection," I say. "Inflammatory."

Everyone looks at me. Even in the dim light, I can see their faces screwed up into question marks.

Meg beckons me to her desk. "What does that mean?" she whispers.

"Rachel can't say I did anything to her dog or phone," I say. "It hasn't been proven yet. She's causing prejudice, Your Honor."

"Good point," Meg says. She shines the flashlight at

Rachel. "You heard her. Don't be inflammatory. There'll be no prejudice in my court." Meg turns the light back to Sofia.

"Whatever," Rachel says. "Okay, Sofia. What was Abigail doing before the hike?"

"She was in the bathroom, puking. I imagine she looked something like this." Sofia opens her mouth, rolls her eyes back so we can only see the whites of her eyes, and makes gagging sounds.

"Shhhh," we all say.

"Come on, Fia," Rachel says. "Get serious. Did you see her doing anything, like, suspicious?"

Sofia, still giggling, shakes her head. "No, when I left, she was still locked in the bathroom."

Rachel leans against the bunk bed. "Why were you the last to leave the cabin?"

"I couldn't find my hoodie. Finally I found it, but then I had to use the bathroom, but couldn't because, you know . . ." Sofia sticks her finger inside her mouth. "So then I ran to the bathroom by the barn."

Rachel nods. "What else did you do today?"

Sofia shrugs. "The same things you guys did. A hike to the lake. Canoed a little. Checked out the fish. Threw a leech at Gabby. Almost fell out of the boat laughing because she went nuts trying to get it off her."

"I could have died," Gabby says. "Those things are like miniature vampires. They'll suck your blood dry."

Sofia turns to Meg. "Your highness?" she asks. "Gabby's not allowed to be talking, right?"

"Oh. Yeah," Meg says. "Quiet over there. I mean, order in the court."

Gabby folds her arms across her chest.

"What happened after the canoe trip?" Rachel asks.

"I hiked to the main camp with Quinn. We borrowed the instant camera from Hock-Eye to look for banana slugs to take photographs. I found a banana slug, and tried to get Quinn to kiss it. But she chickened out at the last second."

I consider raising Quinn's Street Smarts score for recognizing the hygienic repercussions of kissing snails and listen to Sofia explain the rest of her evening.

"Went to dinner, ate three hot dogs. Went to the fire pit, roasted some marshmallows. Sang some stupid songs until Meg started yelling about an ax murderer or something. Then I came back to the cabin with the rest of you guys."

Rachel asks her if she returned to the cabin any other time during the day.

"Nope." Sofia holds up her right hand. "And I swear that's the truth, the whole truth, and nothing but the truth, so help me God."

"Thank you," Rachel says. "I call Gabby to the stand."

Gabby jumps off my bed.

I sigh. "Excuse me, Your Honor, but it's trial procedure for the opposing attorney to cross-examine the witness."

Meg scratches her neck. "Uh . . . uh . . ." she sputters.

"It's my turn to ask Sofia questions," I explain.

"Oh right," Meg says. "Proceed."

Gabby plops back onto my mattress.

I click my heels, put my hands behind my back, and pace the rug. I stop right in front of Sofia and stare her in the eyes. My first question is a zinger: "Why did you want to wear a hoodie on such a warm day?"

"I thought it might be breezy down by the water," Sofia answers, scratching her cheek.

A memory flutters through my brain. Sofia's karate stance, and how she pushed up the short sleeves of her T-shirt. "I don't recall you wearing it when you returned to the cabin this evening."

Sofia shrugs. "I must have left it at the fire pit. I'm always losing that thing."

"Hey," Meg says. "Are you sure you were wearing a hoodie today?"

Sofia nods as she taps her sparkly fingernails against her top lip.

In the moonlight coming through our window, I can see Meg's crinkled face as she stares hard at Sofia, who stares hard at her nails.

"Where did you find your hoodie?" I ask.

Sofia scratches her cheek. "Underneath my bed," she says.

"Did you steal Rachel's phone?" I ask.

She puts her hands in her lap and looks me in the eye. "Nope."

I study Sofia for a few moments. Interesting. She touched her mouth or face the entire time I questioned her, but stopped when I asked about stealing the phone. It's a well-known fact that liars touch their faces or cover their mouths when telling untruths. So she's most likely being honest about the phone. But she's probably hiding something else.

"Come on, Abigail," Rachel says. "We don't have all night."

"No further questions." I walk to the door and stand next to Bailiff Quinn, who's balancing on one leg. The other is bent in a tree pose, her foot pressed against her upper thigh.

Gabby marches to the witness chair. Sofia throws herself onto my bed.

Rachel walks to the open window. As she tries to wave some air into the stuffy room, she rattles off questions for Gabby.

"Did Abigail tell you about my phone?"

"No," Gabby answers.

"Did she ever say she wished she had a phone at camp?"

"No."

"Did you see Abigail try to sneak into my room?"

"No."

Rachel pinches her chin. "What did you do after canoeing in the lake?"

"Meg and I hiked to the barn. We had to set up for dinner."

"Did you come to the cabin before dinner?" Rachel asks.

"No. But I know someone who went to the cabin right *after* dinner."

"Who?"

"Quinn." Gabby points in our direction.

Quinn wobbles in her tree pose.

"Hock-Eye heated up some canned soup for Abigail and asked Quinn to bring it to her," Gabby continues.

"Let's call her to the witness chair next," Sofia says.

I raise my hand. "Excuse me, please. I haven't questioned Gabby yet. And witnesses can't call other witnesses to the stand." These girls are hopeless.

"And I'm the bailiff," Quinn says. "Isn't it, like, a conflict of interest for me to testify in the courtroom I'm in charge of?"

"Fine," Rachel says. "You're fired."

Quinn draws in a breath and makes a noise like her feelings are hurt.

"Gabby, you're bailiff now," Rachel says.

My roommate claps her hands together, jumps out of the chair, and stands next to Quinn at the door.

I approach the desk where Meg sits. "Your Honor, I haven't questioned Gabby yet. Surely this can't be okay with you?"

Meg shrugs. "Sounds good to me. I want to hear what Quinn has to say."

She shines the light on Quinn and swoops it toward the empty chair. "Now sit down, Quinn. Rachel, it's your turn."

I throw my hands in the air. "I give up."

Meg shushes me. Quinn glides to the chair and slumps down in it. Rachel leans against the bunk and crosses her arms.

"Quinn," she says. "What happened when you came back to the cabin and brought Abigail her soup?"

Quinn folds her legs into a butterfly pose. "Nothing. I gave her the soup. She ate it. I left."

Rachel prods her for more details. "Where did Abigail eat the soup?" Quinn points to where Meg sits. "Did she leave her room?" Quinn shakes her head.

"Did you go into *my* room before you left?" Rachel asks.

Quinn crosses her arms. "No, I did not."

"Did you murder Dabney and steal my phone?"

"No." Quinn looks straight into her friend's eyes.

"I'm done." Rachel slides her back down the side of the bunk and sits on the floor.

"Next," Meg says, looking at me.

I take a step toward Quinn. "Did you hurt yourself when you tumbled over that chair?"

Quinn jerks her head and blinks a couple of times. "What chair?"

"You fell, remember? When you were doing yoga in the main room?"

Quinn frowns. "Number one, I never break a yoga pose. Number two, I never fall. Ever."

"But I heard you . . . wait . . . what's that noise?"

A door closes. Meg flicks off the flashlight.

"It's Hock-Eye," Sofia whispers. "Hide!" She throws my covers over herself. I wince, thinking about all the skin cells she's probably leaving behind in my bed.

Meg ducks behind the desk. Quinn leaps out of the chair and climbs into Gabby's bunk.

"Hey, that's my bed," Gabby says as she bounds across the room and scrambles up behind Quinn.

I jerk my head around, looking for a place to go, but there's really nowhere left to hide. Rachel circles the room. She doesn't know what to do either. The doorknob squeaks. Rachel stops her pacing. Someone whimpers. Someone else shushes. I stare at the doorknob and watch it turn.

There's no helping it. I'm going to get caught past lights out. Hock-Eye will barge into my personal space and yell at me for violating the Hollyhock Handbook. A strike will be issued against my good name. I will be sentenced to chicken duty on the farm and risk potential exposure to avian flu. If I were the fainting type, I would collapse from the anxiety.

Fainting! I think. *That's it.*

As the bedroom door opens, I throw myself backward, like Jacqueline Richailbeaux did when she collapsed during the climax of *A Mummy's Love*. I land on Hock-Eye, pushing her back out into the main room. I misjudge her strength, and we end up tumbling straight to the floor. She's surprisingly small.

"Oh là là," I say breathlessly, throwing my arm across my forehead. "*Je suis malade.* I'm sick."

"What the heck are you doing?" She shoves me away from her. That's odd. She doesn't sound like the camp director.

I push myself up on an elbow to see Emmy, not Hock-Eye, getting up from the floor.

"What are you doing here?" I ask.

"What are *you* doing out of bed?" she asks me.

Realizing Emmy could still very well report me to Hock-Eye, I sink back to the floor and moan. "I . . . I . . . was going to get some water, but then I started feeling woozy. I must still be recovering from my earlier illness." I lift my head from the floor to see if I can gauge her reaction. She turns and heads toward my bedroom.

"Wait!" I say. "What are you doing?"

She disappears in the bathroom, which is right next to my room. "Getting you some water," she says. "It's important to stay hydrated when you're sick."

As she turns on the faucet, I scramble off the floor. She returns into the main room and hands me a cup of water. I gulp it down.

She touches my elbow. "Do you need help getting back to bed?"

"No!" I yell, jumping away from her.

Emmy furrows her brow at me.

I look at the now empty cup and set it on the table. "Wow, this water really revived me. I'm feeling better already. I'll just go to sleep now." I walk into my room, spin around, and start pushing the door shut. "Happy Hollyhock dreams," I whisper.

Emmy grabs the door to prevent it from closing.

I hold my breath.

"Feel better," she says. "You don't want to miss the Hollyhock Hunt tomorrow."

I swallow and nod.

She releases the door and turns around. I watch her walk across the wood planks of the main room and out the front door.

When the screen door finally squeaks closed, I release my breath. The rest of the room flutters to life behind me.

Sofia throws off my sheet. "I almost peed my pants I was so scared." She bolts out of the bottom bunk and beelines to the bathroom next door.

Quinn breathes aloud as she climbs down the ladder. "Inhale, exhale, inhale, exhale."

Meg crawls out from underneath the desk. "My sister would freak if she knew I was up past lights out."

"You were amazing, Abigail," Gabby says from the top bunk. "Thanks for covering for us."

Rachel grunts. "Oh please. She was protecting her own butt. Now let's get back to the trial."

Meg stands and brushes off the knees of her plaid pajama bottoms. "Are you nuts? We're lucky we didn't get caught! I'm not taking another chance. Emmy—or worse, Hock-Eye—could come back around!" She marches across the cabin to her own room. "I'm not missing the Hollyhock Hunt!"

"Come on," Rachel says to Quinn, who is also leaving. "What're the chances of that happening?"

"Highly likely," Quinn says.

Rachel groans. She turns around and backs out the door, pointing at me. "Fine. But we're not done here." One bedroom door clicks shut and then another. I push ours closed too.

"That really was awesome what you did with Emmy," Gabby says as she settles in her top bunk. "You totally could have ratted us out. I wouldn't have blamed you if you had. Some of those girls haven't been all that nice to you."

I think back to the times I told Principal Adams about the unflattering names, the intentional shoves, and my numerous hijacked backpacks. "Previous experience has taught me that tattling gets you nowhere, especially with your adversaries," I say. "It can sometimes lead to more vigorous retaliation."

I slip under the sheets and shudder, thinking about all the strange skin cells that now cover my bedclothes. I'm not sure how I'm going to sleep tonight. It's bad enough imagining your own.

I push the sheets down to the end of the bed and lie flat on my back with my arms pressed against my sides. I try to distract myself from thoughts of the tens of thousands of dust mites that must be living in this old mattress. But it's too late. My imagination conjures up an image of an eight-legged hairy, beetle-like creature. I shake my head from side to side trying to shoo it out, but now another image projects onto the back of my eyelids—the creature's underbelly. I sigh. It's going to be a long night.

Date and Time:

Tuesday, June 28, 7:03 a.m.

Location:

Camp Hollyhock, Redwood Shores, California

Description of Activity:

We are preparing for the Hollyhock Hunt, a camp-wide scavenger hunt, where campers pair up to search the grounds for a list of objects. The pairs who finish first, second, and third receive prizes and extra points for the Hollyhock Honor. Except for Subject Meg, the girls in Clovis Cabin don't seem that interested in winning the Hollyhock Honor. Subject Rachel says she doesn't need another one. Subject Sofia calls it "dumb." Subject Quinn says competition isn't healthy for her chakra. And Subject Gabby thinks it's a shame that we all can't receive an honor.

I was hoping that Subject Gabby and I could be partners for the Hollyhock Hunt, but she chose Subject Quinn instead. This means that I have to be paired with Subject Sofia. Our list includes a pinecone, a dandelion seed head, a feather, an acorn, an oak leaf, and some various flowers.

Reflections:

The despair that I recorded in my last entry has dissipated overnight. Though last night's mockery of a mock trial did little to prove my innocence, I was able to convince Subject Gabby that the accusations against me were false. So there is hope yet for my friendship experiment. In addition, I have raised her Sidekick Score 2 points in Advising Capabilities because of some fascinating feedback she provided on "know-it-alls." I had no idea that sharing knowledge could be construed as showing off. Her score is now 23 out of 30.

At this point in my observations, it seems that my roommate will most likely be my new best friend. However, there is another girl I should consider: Subject Meg. Her knowledge of first aid and concussion protocols give her a Street Smarts score of 8. She was an adequate judge during the mock trial so I will award her a 5 for Quiet Listening. Advising Capabilities seem strictly dependent on her sister's experience and knowledge so she receives a 3 here. Total score 16 out of 30. Not a bad start, but she has room for improvement.

Questions:

· Who was the person who tripped over the chair in the common area yesterday evening before the "murder" was discovered? I had assumed it had been Subject Quinn, but the trial uncovered that it was someone else. Is this clumsy person the thief?

Future Actions:

Continue evaluating Subjects Meg and Gabby to ensure I establish the most appropriate match for my experiment. Also work on proving my innocence in regard to the theft of Subject Rachel's phone.

"What the heck are you doing?" Sofia shrieks at me. "You can't pick poppies! Everyone knows it's illegal! You're gonna get us arrested!"

"Contrary to popular belief, picking California poppies is not always illegal," I say, plucking the orange flower from the hundreds just like it growing along the hillside in front of us.

"Yeah, it is," Sofia says. "We can't pick the ones at school."

"That's because your school is on public property, not private, like Camp Hollyhock." I slide the poppy into the brown paper bag that already holds some crumbling leaves, a pinecone, and a dandelion seed head. "The California Penal Code 384a dictates that a person shall not willfully or negligently cut, destroy, mutilate, or remove plant material that is growing upon state or county highway rights-of-way. A person shall not willfully or negligently cut—"

"Okay, okay, I get it," Sofia interrupts.

"You didn't let me get to the part that applies to us. Where was I? Oh yes. A person shall not willfully or negligently cut, destroy, mutilate, or remove plant material that is growing upon public land or upon land that is not his or hers without a written permit from the owner of the land, signed by the owner of the land or the owner's authorized agent." I hold up the list of items we are required to retrieve for our outdoor scavenger hunt. "Though not notarized, this paper given to us by Hock-Eye should suffice as a written permit. If she didn't want us to pick her poppies, she shouldn't have included them on our list."

"Let me try to understand something here." Sofia plants her hands on her hips. "You've read and memorized this California Plant Whatever Code?"

"Of course. It's important to know when and where it's appropriate to fell a tree or pull a plant."

Sofia stares at me for several seconds. Finally she shakes her head. "Hurl Girl, you take geek to a whole new level."

I study Sofia's words. Was that a compliment or an insult? Here's another opportunity to retest my theory about Opposite Day Behavior.

"And you're an idiot."

Sofia's eyelids flutter up and down, and her mouth drops open. "Thanks a lot, *bonehead*."

It worked! I even received a compliment in return, cleverly disguised as an insult. Fascinating. "You're not welcome," I say.

Since this Opposite Day Behavior seems to indicate we're hitting it off, I'll continue measuring her Sidekick Score.

Her Quiet Listening numbers are unfortunately low, but maybe she'll fare better in the Thoughtful Advice category. I review the items we still need to locate for our scavenger hunt. "Where do you think we should go to look for feathers?"

"Go look for them yourself, jerk," she says.

Oh my. She's really overdoing it with the compliments.

"I could really use some help from a dunderhead like you," I reply. "Should we look for empty snail shells instead?"

"Leave me alone." Sofia starts jogging toward a patch of sequoias.

I follow her as she loops through the trees. "Good idea. Snails do prefer moist areas."

While Sofia kicks leaves with her boots, I squat closer to the ground for a bug's-eye view. After a few minutes, the sounds of swishing foliage stop. I look up and see Sofia sitting on a tree stump.

"Where should we go next?" I ask.

"I have an idea where you can go," she snaps.

"The lake?" I ask.

She scoffs. "Yeah, right. Go jump in the lake."

"Another good, I mean *rotten*, idea," I say. I stand up and head down the hiking trail to the lake.

A few hundred feet down the path, I come across Rachel, crouched behind a manzanita bush. Instead of scouring the ground or combing the bright green leaves for one of the scavenger items, she stoops motionless as if concealing herself. I instinctively duck. Is there a coyote or a mountain lion out there? I swallow. *Please don't let it be a grizzly bear!* I creep over to her.

Rachel turns and holds a finger to her lips.

"What are we hiding from?" I whisper.

Rachel points through the branches at a figure pacing between two eucalyptus trees. Standing on two feet, it reaches about four and a half feet high. Its brown mane flops as it turns to zero in on something in the distance.

"It's a boy!" I say.

"Shhhh," Rachel hisses.

"What's he doing here?" I whisper.

"He probably snuck over here from Camp Huckleberry, the boys' camp on the other side of the lake," she whispers.

I begin to straighten into a standing position. "I'm going to get Hock-Eye. This is an all-girls camp. No boys allowed!"

"Oh my God," Rachel says. "Look!"

I crouch back down.

It's Quinn. She steals between the trees and shrubs. She spots the brown-haired boy and freezes for a moment. She looks around, then approaches him.

The boy rolls his shoulders back to make himself taller. He manages to reach Quinn's shoulder. He flicks his neck back, flopping his hair over to the other side of his head. "Hey," he says.

"Hey," she says.

He stuffs his hands in his pockets. "I was starting to think you wouldn't show."

Rachel sucks in a breath. "That must be Jason," she whispers.

"Who's that?" I ask.

"Quinn's boyfriend," Rachel answers.

We turn to face each other and then look back out at the lovebirds.

Quinn crosses her arms and sticks her hip out. "Well, I'm here, aren't I?"

"Yeah, but you never texted me back yesterday," he says. "Why'd you go dark?"

I turn to look at Rachel. Her jaw is clenched, and she stares at Quinn icily. "Did Quinn bring her phone too?" I whisper.

Rachel doesn't respond.

"Outlook not so good, dude!" Quinn groans, looking up at the sky. "I told you not to text me back. You're gonna get us in trouble!"

The boy reaches out to touch her arm. "Chill. We're not going to get caught."

Quinn jerks away. "Uh, very doubtful. That phone I used wasn't mine."

Rachel stands up suddenly. "Whose phone was it?" she yells.

Quinn's head whips around. Her eyes widen when she sees Rachel.

The boy shrieks and starts to run. He almost rams right into Gabby, who has just emerged from the trees. He shrieks again and runs in the opposite direction, weaving around trunks, never looking back.

"What the heck was that?" Gabby asks.

"Quinn's boyfriend," I say, standing up from my crouch.

"She has a boyfriend?" Gabby asks. "That's so cool."

Something rustles on the path behind us. It's Sofia, kicking the dried leaves on the ground as she walks toward us. "Who has a boyfriend?" she asks.

"Quinn does," Rachel says coldly. "His name is Jason." Rachel stomps around the bush and beelines toward Quinn.

We all follow her. "And you used my phone to text him, didn't you?"

Quinn gives a slow, tiny nod.

"I didn't get a good look," Gabby says, "but he seemed super cute."

"We should call them Quinnson," Sofia says.

Rachel storms into Quinn's personal space. "So you're the one who stole it?"

Quinn shakes her head. She covers her face with her hands.

"Excuse me," I say. "My mother tells me it's not polite to say 'I told you so.' However, I *did* tell you so." I look around, expecting words of apology and remorse. But it's just crickets. Literally. The bugs chirp among the bushes.

We all watch Quinn as she whimpers behind her fingers.

"I can't believe you'd do this to me," Rachel says coldly.

"And me," I add, trying to be just as frosty. "Letting me take the blame for a crime I didn't commit." I cross my arms and turn my back on Quinn. Still, nobody says a word. I glance over my shoulder. Where is the moral outrage over my unfair treatment?

Quinn snuffles. "I just wanted to talk to Jason. We've been boyfriend-girlfriend for two months and—"

"That's, like, forever," Gabby says, twirling a lock of hair around her finger.

Quinn nods and wipes her nose with the back of her wrist. "I know, right?"

"Seriously," Rachel moans. "Are you kidding me right now? You destroy my dog, steal my phone—"

"And sully my good name," I interject.

Rachel frowns at me and continues, "—because of a two-month relationship?"

"My reply is no." Quinn wipes her eyes. "I just used the phone for a few seconds to text him to meet me here."

"Why didn't you just ask me?" Rachel says. "I would have let you borrow it. You didn't have to steal it."

"But I didn't. I just sent one text and then returned the phone to Dabney. I left him on your pillow, just like I found him. That's the truth."

"Hey, Rachel!" someone calls from the hiking path. It's Meg. "What are you doing sitting around? You're supposed to be scavenging."

"I took a break," Rachel says.

"You can't take breaks during the Hollyhock Hunt!" Meg yells. "I want those extra points for the Hollyhock Honor. What've you found so far?"

"Nada," Rachel says.

Meg's mouth drops open. "What have you been doing all this time?"

"She's still trying to figure out what happened to her phone," Gabby explains.

"The phone again!" Meg says, exasperated. "Are you kidding me? This is camp, not *CSI Special Device Unit*."

"Chill out," Rachel says. "The Hollyhock Hunt's just a dumb game."

"A game I want to win. And it's not dumb." Meg waves her arms around. "Now get scavenging."

Rachel rolls her eyes and stomps off. Quinn jogs after her and grabs Rachel's arm. "Are we cool?" she asks. "I didn't destroy Dabney or steal your phone. Do you believe me?"

"NOW!" Meg shrieks.

"All right, all right!" Quinn yells back. She closes her eyes, takes a deep breath, and lets it out. "But seriously, Meg, this energy you're spewing is *so* toxic."

We all head in separate directions. Sofia and I continue down the hiking trail to the lake. Meg and Rachel head the opposite way toward the hillside of poppies. And Quinn and Gabby tramp back into the grove of eucalyptus trees.

When we meet the others back at the barn about thirty minutes later, we discover that Meg and Rachel finished third in the scavenger hunt. Though disappointed she didn't come in first, Meg was quite pleased to receive extra points for tracking down the Hollyhock Hunt's special bonus find: rattlesnake skin.

Hock-Eye calls Meg up to the barn stage and hands her a special badge. Meg addresses the entire camp from the platform. "I bet you didn't know each time a rattlesnake sheds its skin, a new rattle is added to its tail."

According to the Chore Chart, I'm on lunchtime dish duty with Rachel. After a meal of hot dogs and salad, she and I head to the working kitchen in the back corner of the barn. Rachel fills the large stainless steel sink with water. I wait for her to apologize for her false accusations. But the apology doesn't come.

I clear my throat. "Is there something you want to say to me?"

She points at the dishwashing soap on the counter. "Can you hand me that?"

I pass her the plastic container. "I think the words you are looking for are 'I'm sorry.'"

She squeezes the bottle and watches the orange liquid pour into the water. "What do I have to be sorry for?"

"For accusing me of murdering your dog and stealing your phone." I pull on a pair of blue plastic gloves.

"I'm still not sure it *wasn't* you." She places the soap on the counter, grabs a stack of dirty plastic dishes, and dumps them in the soapy water.

"Even after what Quinn told you this morning?" I ask. "How can you still believe that I had anything to do with it when she has readily admitted to using your phone?"

"But she also said she put it back on my pillow." She plunges her hands into the water, grabs a dish, and scrubs it with a sponge. "I've never known her to lie to me."

"Even though she kept the real truth from you for an entire day?"

"Yeah, that doesn't look good, does it?" Rachel sighs, and continues scrubbing the dish.

After about ninety seconds of furious cleansing, I hold out my hand. "I do appreciate a thorough cleaning, but I think you've done all you can for that plate."

She pushes the dripping dish into my gloved hand. "So do you think she did it? That she took my phone and is lying about putting it back where she found it?"

I wipe the plastic dry with a dish towel and consider Rachel's question. I really don't know if Quinn's telling the truth or not. As a scientist, I hate to make a judgment when there are so many unknowns. Instead, I say, "For my own benefit, I know I should tell you yes. But the truth is, I have my doubts."

"Why?"

"For one thing," I say, "last night when you asked Quinn if she murdered Dabney and stole your phone, she looked you straight in the eye and said 'No.'" I demonstrate by looking deep into Rachel's eyes.

Rachel shifts her gaze down to the sink of dirty dishes. "So what?" she asks.

I place my dry plate on the counter. "Many psychological studies show that liars shift their eyes when telling untruths. Since she was not afraid to look at you directly, that leads me to believe that she did leave the phone and an intact Dabney on your pillow, like she said."

"Okay," Rachel says, handing me another dish. "Is there a second thing?"

I nod, grabbing another plate to dry. "Last night after Quinn gave me the soup, I thought I heard her trip in the common room. But when I asked her about it later, she looked me in the eye and, without fidgeting, said it wasn't her. So that means someone else must have entered the cabin after Quinn delivered the soup and before Meg returned."

Another memory suddenly comes into focus. "I just realized somebody else may have entered the cabin yesterday," I say.

"Who?" Rachel asks.

"I don't know. I was lying in bed, recovering from my gastrointestinal troubles. One arm was over my eyes like this." I set the plate down on the small stack growing on the counter next to us and dangle my forearm across my face. "So I couldn't see who it was. At the time, I thought it was Sofia, but now that I think about it, because of the footsteps, it couldn't have been."

"Because of the footsteps?" Rachel repeats.

"I only heard seven." I bring down my elbow. "I would need to go back and map this out, but—"

"Wait." Rachel raises her hand. "You're telling me that you remember exactly how many footsteps you heard yesterday while lying in bed sick?"

"Yes. Probably three steps to your room and then maybe four back out."

"That is so weird."

"Exactly! Because Sofia is on the shorter side, she should have taken more steps to get to her room, especially since it's farther from the front door than yours. So that means—"

"No. I mean it's weird that you remember all this random stuff. The way Quinn answered a question last night and how many footsteps you heard yesterday."

I shrug. "As I told you when we first met, my brain has the capability to store massive amounts of information."

"I could use a brain like that." Rachel points to her head.

"It has its drawbacks too."

"Like what?" She wipes her wet hands on her jeans shorts.

"My memory coupled with my exceptional cognitive skills have pushed me ahead academically."

"Is that a fancy way of saying you skipped a grade?"

"I've skipped three grades."

Rachel's eyes widen. "So after the summer, you'll be going into . . ." She drops the plate she was scrubbing back into the sink, and counts on her fingers. "Tenth grade?"

I nod.

"That's awesome!" she says. "In, like, three years, you'll totally be done with the high-school scene and off to party it up in college. How the heck is that bad?"

"Because I don't have friends in high school. You would think older students would be interested in conversing in French, attending an exhibition of Mayan artifacts at the local museum, or debating the theory of everything."

Rachel raises her eyebrows. "You would think."

"But they're not. And since I've been separated from girls my own age for so long, I'm not really sure how to connect with them, either. I may have a high intelligent quotient, offers of acceptance to prestigious summer programs from Ivy League colleges, and a bright future ahead of me in anthropology, archaeology, or whatever field I choose to study, but it's lonely at the top, as they say." I move the stack of clean plates to a cupboard by the kitchen entrance. "I was hoping to change that this summer."

Rachel drains the water in the sink. "How's it working out so far?"

"I'm having moderate success, but your false accusations are certainly not helping matters."

"I don't think that's your only problem," she mutters.

"What do you mean?"

Rachel shakes the water off her hands, takes a breath, and steps closer to me. I can tell she's about to impart important information, so I fight my instinct to step back. "How about we make a deal?" she asks.

"What kind of deal?"

She puts her arm around me. "Abigail, Abby, my little Abbyologist, how about you and your Ivy League brain figure out who stole my phone, and I'll tell everybody you had nothing to do with it?"

Her soggy hand rests on the upper part of my arm,

a flagrant violation of the personal space rule. I shrug my arm to try to shake it off. My efforts fail. "But you already know I'm not responsible," I say, "so you can just clarify the situation with the girls now."

"Well, *technically speaking*," Rachel says, making air quotes with her free hand, "I don't know that for sure. So I would feel much better clearing your name when I have the entire truth." She pats my arm.

I push her away from me. "This isn't a deal. This is blackmail!"

"Whatever," she says. "So, are we good or what?"

I fling my dish towel onto the counter. "Nothing about this situation is good."

The nerve! It's hard to imagine that when I first arrived in Clovis Cabin, I thought we had a chance of being friends.

Rachel shrugs. "If I were you, I'd get busy," she says as she heads out of the kitchen.

Date and Time:

Wednesday, June 29, 7:12 a.m.

Location:

Camp Hollyhock, Redwood Shores, California

Description of Activity:

On today's agenda is the Fourteenth Annual Hollympics. Soon the entire camp will meet at the meadow behind the barn. There, the cabins will compete against one another in a series of games and activities that include tug-of-war, relay races, and a hula-hoop contest. The top three cabins receive medals and extra points for the Hollyhock Honor. Though lukewarm about the Hollyhock Honor, the inhabitants of Clovis Cabin are red-hot and fired up for winning the Hollympics. At stake are bragging rights and ultimate glory for the winning cabin. Everyone seems to have their game faces on today.

Reflections:

My status within the cabin has improved slightly after Subject Quinn became a person of interest in the intrigue involving Subject Rachel's stolen phone.

Subject Rachel no longer believes I'm culpable but refuses to publicly exonerate me. Thus Subject Sofia, who always follows Subject Rachel's lead, continues to think I'm responsible for the crimes in our cabin. This is unfortunate because we bonded briefly during the Hollyhock Hunt yesterday. (Also of note is Subject Sofia's Opposite Day Behavior. I must keep this conduct in mind when interacting with her.) Though it vexes me that Subject Sofia takes her friend's word over the facts, I must acknowledge that this is an appropriate anthropological response. As hunter-gatherers, our social standing within the herd was deemed more important to survival than our ability to accept reason.[1]

Social ranking also explains why Subject Quinn is so preoccupied with remedying her strained relationship with Subject Rachel instead of making amends with me. Since yesterday morning, Subject Quinn has apologized numerous times to Subject Rachel for her deception. Subject Rachel's responses have included shrugs, eye rolls, and one gruff *"Okay!"* My observations indicate that Subject Rachel is showing her displeasure to Subject Quinn by giving her the silent treatment, punishing someone for a perceived wrong by refusing communication. Subject Quinn has been in misery. If she hadn't allowed me to shoulder the blame for the theft, I would almost feel sorry for her. Almost.

Subject Meg doesn't seem to care one way or another about my innocence, the feud between Subjects Rachel and Quinn, or the fate of the phone. She seems focused only on winning the Hollyhock Honor. As she has informed us many, many, *many* times, her older sister is a two-time winner and Subject Meg feels she must follow in those footsteps. She is well on her way to achieving this accomplishment. Not only did she do well in the Hollyhock Hunt, but she also received extra Hollyhock Honor points for making not one but two God's-eyes, a craft we did yesterday afternoon that involves wrapping yarn over and under a cross made out of two sticks.

Subject Gabby has remained my trusty ally in this debacle, and the experiment is proving that she could indeed be my best match. While she was weaving her God's-eye yesterday, she made time to advise me on how to neatly tie and trim a knot in the yarn to make it practically invisible. Her Sidekick Score has risen 2 points. One point for the helpful craft advice, and 1 point for quietly listening as I spoke about the history of fencing during last evening's dinner. She now has a Sidekick Score of 25 out of 30.

Most of the girls' scores have remained the same:

Subject Meg: 16

Subject Rachel: 8

Subject Sofia: 4

Quinn's has been reduced to 8. I had to kick her Street Smarts score back to 0 because she a.) broke the Number One Rule of the Girl Code: Sisters Before Misters,[2] and b.) allowed herself to be exposed during a clandestine meeting with said Mister.

Future Action:

Since employing Opposite Day Behavior worked so well with Sofia, try it out on the other subjects in the cabin and see if my social standing improves.

Endnotes:

1. Source: *Young Anthropologist*, Special Holiday Issue

2. Source: "Top Ten Rules of the Girl Code," Sparklegirl website

A warm wind blows the minty aroma of eucalyptus across the meadow as we prepare for our first event in the Hollympics, the tug-of-war. Clovis Cabin forms a semicircle around the end of a thick, fraying rope. The inhabitants of Laguna Cabin gather around the other end. "Good luck, Laguna," I say with a wave.

Nobody from Laguna waves or wishes us luck in return. One of the girls points two fingers at her eyes and then back at us. Sofia responds by growling at them like an attack dog. It doesn't appear like this competition is going to be a friendly one.

"I bet you didn't know that tug-of-war used to be an actual Olympic sport," Meg says, picking up our end of the rope from the rocky ground.

"Indeed, that is true," I say, impressed with her knowledge of history. "From 1900 to 1920 it was—"

"I bet you didn't know that we really don't care," Sofia interrupts. Her Sidekick Score isn't improving.

"Did you know rope climbing used to be an Olympic sport too?" I ask Meg.

She nods. "And croquet."

"Stop yapping and get organized!" Rachel says, grabbing the rope from Meg. "I want to win this." Rachel arranges us with tallest toward the middle of the rope and shortest at the end.

"This is height discrimination!" Meg calls from the back of the line. "I may be small, but I'm super strong."

"Stay where you are, Meg!" Rachel yells as she takes her place toward the front of our line, behind Quinn. "We're gonna start any second."

Meg stomps in frustration. She releases the rope and marches up to Quinn. "I belong up front."

Quinn signals for Meg to go back to the end of the line just as Hock-Eye blows an air horn, which is the Hollympics "Go" signal. With only one hand on the rope, Quinn doesn't have a firm grip, and Laguna Cabin defeats us in less than five seconds. We all tumble down and get dragged across the dried grass, the first cabin to cave.

"I told you!" Meg yells. "I should've been closer to the front."

"Yeah, that's exactly why we lost to those Laguna losers," Sofia says, extracting a twig from her dark curls. "Not because you left your post to have a major meltdown!"

The next event is a relay race, where we run back and forth across the field balancing an egg on a spoon. Rachel takes charge and coaches us on how to run a successful relay. "You need to make sure the large part of the egg is centered in the large part of spoon," she says as she pulls her dark shiny hair through a hair band. "Also take big, slow steps instead of small, fast ones."

"Are you sure about this?" Meg asks. "My sister, who's a two-time—"

"Shut it about your sister!" Rachel yells. She thrusts a spoon into Meg's hand. "Now go!"

Meg scowls but grabs the spoon. She, Gabby, and Quinn take their places on the other side of the meadow. At the sound of the air horn, Sofia races cautiously toward them, an egg balanced on her spoon in the manner that Rachel suggested.

Rachel and I watch Sofia cross the field and transfer the egg to Quinn's spoon. Quinn's long legs scissor across the meadow. Rachel cups her hands around her mouth. "Watch out for that hole, Quinn!" She clenches her fists in anticipation, then pumps them in the air once Quinn maneuvers around the obstruction. "Woo-hoo!"

Rachel hands me a spoon. I'm the next to race after Quinn. "Do you have any last-minute advice before I go out there?" I ask her.

"Don't take your eyes off that egg," she says. "If it falls

off the spoon, you have to come back to the starting line and do it all over again."

"Okay, got it," I say.

Quinn and I successfully transfer the egg, and I'm off trekking across the meadow. I keep my eyes glued to the egg. To keep laser-sharp focus, I repeat the word over and over in my head. *Egg. Egg. Egg.* Egg translates to *ovus* in Latin. *Ovus. Ovus. Ovus.* Which is why we call an egg-shaped object an oval. *Oval. Oval. Oval.*

The girls are yelling, so I must still be in the lead. My heart pounds as I continue focusing on the oval, oval, oval. An oval is not the same as an ellipse, ellipse, ellipse. An ellipse has a precise mathematical definition. An oval does not. An ellipse always has two axes. An oval usually has one. An ellipse is used in geometry. An oval is not. An ellipse will always be an oval. An oval is not always an ellipse. Which should not be confused with the ellipsis, which are the three dots that in written conversation indicate a pause in speech. Dot. Dot. Dot.

Now the girls are yelling for me. "Abigail! Abigail! Go Abbyologist!"

Though I want to look and watch them cheer, I can't take my eyes off the egg, egg, egg.

"Stop! Turn right! Get out of the way!" someone shouts.

Wait. What?

I finally look up from the egg. Claire from Ponderosa Cabin is heading straight toward me with her own egg balancing on a spoon. I stop before she rams right into me. Somehow I've veered diagonally into their relay race. Curses! I turn to the right to see Gabby and Sofia beckoning me.

"Hurry, hurry!" they shriek.

I right my course. This time I flick my eyes back and forth between the egg and my cabinmates, which slows my pace. Just as I'm carefully tipping my egg into Gabby's spoon, cheers ring out from across the field. Hock-Eye announces the winner. And it's not us. Obviously.

Rachel, Meg, and Quinn run over to us. Rachel bursts my personal space bubble and thrusts her face into mine so that our noses are almost touching. "What the heck happened out there?"

"So very sorry," I say, taking a step back. "I was just doing what you said. I kept both eyes glued to the egg so it wouldn't fall."

Rachel groans. "I didn't mean for you to look at the egg *only*. You were also supposed to keep an eye on Gabby so you could see where to head for the hand-off."

"Oh," I say, rubbing the back of my neck. "Well, you didn't make that clear."

Rachel's face flames a fiery red. "Uggghhh!" she yells before turning around so quickly, I have to dodge her ponytail.

"And you're supposed to be some super genius?" Sofia asks, shaking her head.

"My sources say no," Quinn says.

"Thanks a lot, Abigail," says Meg, who seems to have forgotten that she was the sole reason we lost the last event.

Even Gabby throws a look of disappointment my way as she turns to follow the rest of my cabinmates to our next event, archery. I walk behind them as they trudge toward a pair of red, white, and blue targets set up in the corner of the meadow.

When we arrive at the archery station, Emmy, who's manning the event, tells us only two members of Clovis Cabin will compete this time. "So who's good with a bow and arrow?" she asks.

Meg raises her hand. Emmy hands her a container of arrows and a bow and shows her where to stand. The rest of us sit down on some logs to watch, safely out of range of any potential misfires.

Emmy begins to demonstrate how to hold the bow. "If I were you, I'd—"

"I know what I'm doing," Meg says, waving her off.

Emmy raises her eyebrows but says nothing as she backs away from Meg.

Meg stands as tall as she can, pulls back the bowstring to her chin, and releases the arrow. It flies straight into the red center of the target.

We all clap in amazement.

"I bet you didn't know I'm an expert archer," Meg says.

She repeats the same movements five times, acquiring four bull's-eyes.

Sofia bounds off the logs. "I can do that too," she exclaims, grabbing the bow and arrow set from Meg.

During Sofia's first try, cheers erupt from the tug-of-war station about fifty feet behind her, just as she's releasing her arrow. It zooms over the targets and into the trees.

Sofia turns around and glares at the offending noise.

She tries again, blinking at the sweat dripping into her eyes. This arrow manages to make contact, but with the ground. "I can't see," she whines.

None of Sofia's arrows get close to the target. Meg smolders as they return their archery supplies to Emmy.

"Good try, Sofia," Emmy says. "Next time, try a wider stance."

"Archery is a dumb sport, anyway," Sofia pouts. "No balls, no running."

Quinn fans herself with her cootie catcher. "At least we can head to the shade now."

We walk toward a massive oak tree in the center of the meadow. This is where we'll participate in the hula-hoop contest. All six of us will compete while a counselor times us. Our group's winning time will be compared with those of the other cabins. Whoever can keep their hoops flying high the longest wins.

Quinn slips a hoop over her head and starts swinging her hips. "Don't worry ladies," she says. "I got this. Outlook: gold medal."

"I'm quite good at this too," I say, grabbing another hoop that is leaning against the oak's trunk.

I discovered hula-hooping while participating in a demonstration at our local science museum when I was five years old. The instructor directed us to plant our feet, place the hoop in the small of our backs, and move our pelvises back and forth. At the time, it seemed like magic when I let go of the hoop and it didn't crash to the ground. But I learned that the secret behind the hula-hoop is better than sorcery. It's simple physics! My waist brushing against the hoop creates friction, which fights the gravitational force that pulls the hula-hoop down.

I still enjoy producing the magic of physics with a simple swing of my hips. I have actually grown quite good at it, especially when my mind is focused on something else, like reading. My best time is thirty-six minutes and twenty-one seconds. While reading Shakespeare, thank you very much.

I have no book to read today, but my brain has a figurative library of materials from which to choose. Let's see. Poetry is a nice accompaniment to hooping. The verse's beat will work nicely with the hoop's tiny interior beads that shake like a tambourine as they knock against my waist. I close my eyes, pull up my favorite Roald Dahl poems, and start reading.

Augustus Gloop! Augustus Gloop! The great big greedy nincompoop!

After Augustus, I go through the other poems from *Charlie and the Chocolate Factory*—Violet Beauregarde and then Mike Teavee. Finally I get to Veruca Salt—my favorite.

Down goes Veruca! Down the drain! And here perhaps we should explain—

I open my eyes. All the girls from Clovis Cabin—all the girls at Camp Hollyhock—are gawking at me.

That she will meet, as she descends—

Curses! Have I been reciting these poems out loud this whole time? I freeze. The hoop bangs on the ground.

Oh. No.

I look down. I've just messed up another event. My cabinmates will never forgive me. No one will want to be friends with a two-time loser.

The girls from Clovis Cabin scream. It's worse than I thought! They barrel toward me, arms outstretched. I try to flee in the opposite direction, but the girls are too quick.

They close in, throw their limbs around me, and yell some more as they squeeze me tightly. I cover my head with my arms to protect it as best I can.

"Abigail is awesome!"

"Abbyologist is the hula queen!"

"She beat the camp record!"

"I told you! Outlook: gold medal! We won!"

I drop my arms. "We won?" I ask.

"Yes!" they all shriek. And then the jumping starts. I squeal, convinced I'm about to be trampled to death. They squeal in response and jump faster. Oddly all the frantic movement keeps me from falling. After a few moments, it's over, and the girls disperse as quickly as they pounced.

I believe I've just experienced my first group hug. Thankfully, I have emerged unscathed. I gulp in some air, fan myself with my hat, and am surprised to hear myself laughing. I touch my lips. Did I really enjoy that? The sweat? The skin? The hair? The screaming? My heart pounds in an I-just-made-it-through-a-killer-calculus-test kind of way. I think I feel elated.

"Abigail! Hurry up!" Gabby beckons me from across the field. I run toward her and the rest of the girls, who are already lining up for the sack races. In our final Hollympic event, all fifteen cabins line up on one side of the meadow. Each girl will take a turn jumping across the field and back in a brown burlap bag.

Gabby is the first in our cabin to go. Halfway across the field, she trips and falls. She gets out of her sack to pull herself off the ground.

"What the heck are you doing?" Meg shrieks at her. "You have to remain in the bag at all times! Those are the rules! Now we're disqualified!"

"I didn't know that!" Gabby yells back.

After watching the sack race from the edge of the meadow like a bunch of toddlers in time out, we tramp to the barn with the entire camp for the medal presentation and postgame lunch. Clovis Cabin receives two medals: gold for the hula-hoop contest and silver for archery. Laguna Cabin receives the most medals and is crowned the winner of the Fourteenth Annual Hollympics.

After the awards, Clovis Cabin is uncharacteristically quiet as we eat lunch. Except for Meg. Our mediocre performance infuriates her. "My sister's Hollympics team won a medal in every event last year," she grumbles from the end of our table.

"Who's your sister again?" Rachel asks through a mouth of trail mix.

Meg doesn't answer right away. "Madeline," she says in a quiet voice.

"Huh," Rachel says, chewing thoughtfully. "I don't remember her."

Directly across from me, Sofia pushes around the baked beans on her plate. "Stupid Hollympics," she grumbles. I can tell from her Opposite Day Behavior that she indeed feels fondness for these games.

I nod in agreement. "Quite."

Meg pounds her tiny fist on the table. "They are not stupid!" she yells.

Ah yes. I forgot that Meg doesn't recognize ODB. I must remember to observe her more and find out why. In the meantime, I will have to translate for her. "Meg, I think you misunderstand Sofia. What she means is that she finds the Hollympics—"

Sofia interrupts me. "Dumb, pointless, and fake. And I bet that sister of yours is too!"

Meg gasps. She stands from the table and grabs her plate. "My sister is not fake!" she yells, stomping her little foot.

The barn goes quiet. Chairs rustle and squeak as Hollyhockers strain their necks to see who's making all the noise.

Emmy, who sits with the other counselors at the neighboring table, leans back toward us. "Everything okay over here, Clovis?"

Meg's face reddens. "Everything's just fine," she mumbles. She turns on her heel and storms out of the barn. The campers return to scarfing down their lunches.

Emmy gets up from the table of counselors and follows Meg outside.

"Sofia, Meg actually believes you really meant all those things," I say.

She shrugs. "I don't care." The way Sofia glances at the barn's exit and back at her plate signals to me that she's exhibiting Opposite Day Behavior again. Sofia does care. She shrugs. "It's just so irritating the way she goes on and on about that stupid Hollyhock Honor. She acts likes she's competing in the World Cup or something." She elbows Rachel, who's sitting next to her. "Speaking of which, Mexico beat Brazil in the knockout round on Monday."

As Sofia describes the game-winning goal to Rachel, something occurs to me. I wait until Sofia is finished with her story about the soccer match.

"Oh wow," Gabby says. "That does sound amazing."

I wipe my mouth with a paper napkin. "How did you see what happened at the World Cup on Monday?" I ask.

Sofia freezes. She stuffs another bite of beans into her mouth.

Rachel looks up from her own plate and across the table at me. She swivels in her seat to face her neighbor. "Yeah, Fia, how did you see the game?"

Sofia swallows her beans. "Actually," she says, "I just remembered. I didn't see it." She refuses to look at Rachel.

"Then how were you able to describe that goal in such great detail?" I ask.

Sofia scratches her nose with a perfect pink fingernail. It's a wonder they all managed to survive today's competition without a chip or scratch. "Uh, someone must have told me," she says.

"Who?" Rachel asks.

"I can't remember," Sofia says. "Who cares, anyway?" She pushes the remaining food around on her plate.

Gabby twirls her hair through her fingers. "I didn't even realize World Cup had started. It's so weird without our phones, not knowing what's going on outside Camp Holly—" Gabby's eyes widen.

"Trouble ahead," Quinn says.

Everyone stares at Sofia.

Sofia looks up from her plate at us. "What?" Her eyes dart from face to face. "It's like I said, someone told me about the goal. They just described it in such great . . . uh . . . detail that I felt like I actually saw it in person. But I totally didn't."

I point the end of my fork at Sofia. "So you can remember the description of the game but not the talented storyteller who described it to you? That seems odd."

Sofia shrugs. "Not really. My memory isn't that good. I'm always forgetting stuff."

Rachel nods slowly. "That's true. Sofia does forget stuff. A lot." Rachel raises her eyebrows at me and tilts her head. "Remember she told us how she forgot her hoodie in the cabin the other day instead of bringing it with her on the hike?"

Sofia's face seems to melt with relief as she points to her friend. "Yes, that's true. I didn't have my hoodie on the hike." She turns her palms to the sky and shrugs. "See, I forget stuff all the time. I should seriously be called Sofia-getful." She grins at us. "Get it?"

Rachel slams her hand on the table. Gabby and Sofia jump in their chairs.

Quinn sets down her cootie catcher. "Outlook not so good."

I lean back in my chair. "You told us you were late for the hike because you were looking for the hoodie, which you said you found underneath the bed."

Sofia bites her lip.

"What were you really doing in the cabin, Fia?" Rachel asks.

"My sources say . . . ," Quinn says as she leans over the table toward Sofia, ". . . ripping Dabney's head off."

Sofia jabs a finger in Quinn's face. "I did nothing to that dog!" she hisses.

"But what about the phone?" I whisper, glancing at the table of counselors just a few feet away. They're all giggling and talking together. They don't seem to notice the storm brewing at our table.

Sofia droops her head. Her curls tumble around her

face, coming dangerously close to skimming the dredges of baked beans on her plate.

"I just borrowed it to check the game," she says, her voice a little muffled underneath all the hair. "After I checked the highlights, I hid it back inside Dabney and put him on Rachel's pillow."

Rachel drums her fingers on the table. "It seems just a little too convenient that your story sounds exactly like Quinn's."

Sofia sits up, and her curls fly around her head. "But it's the truth. I didn't destroy Dabney or steal the . . ." she flings her head from side to side, to see if any of the other tables of girls are listening to us. ". . . The you-know. If I had it, I would totally give it to you." Sofia grabs Rachel's hands. "Please, Rachel," she says. "You have to believe me."

Rachel jerks her hands away. "How am I supposed to believe you? You took my phone without asking and then lied to me about it." She turns to glare at Quinn. "And you too."

Quinn looks down at her cootie catcher.

"You guys are supposed to be my friends," Rachel says. "And friends don't steal from each other."

"But I didn't steal it," Sofia says. "I just borrowed it."

"Same here," Quinn says. "You let us use it last summer. I didn't think it was a big deal."

"And I was going to tell you I used it," Sofia continues, "but then it got stolen and I didn't know what to do. I guess I panicked. I'm sorry I lied before, but I'm telling the truth now. I swear."

Rachel grabs her plate and stands up. "I just can't anymore." She stomps off toward the bussing area to dump her plate.

Sofia goes back to pushing cold beans across her plate.

Quinn closes her eyes and does some deep breathing.

"I have a question for you, Quinn," I say. "When did you text Jason? Before or after the hike?"

"Before," she says, her eyes still closed. "I watched Sofia leave, and then I snuck in. You were sleeping." She takes a long breath and lets it out.

"Yes, that makes sense. Longer legs, less footsteps." I shrug. "It's a shame you guys kept the truth from Rachel. It will be hard for her to believe anything you say now."

Sofia grunts. "Thanks for the words of wisdom, Abigail." Her scowl implies she's practicing Opposite Day Behavior.

I respond in kind: "You're quite welcome."

I stand up from the table, walk over to the compost bin to dump my remaining lunch, and leave my plate on the growing dirty stack. Was Sofia also employing ODB when she kept the truth from Rachel? If sharing secrets is a true sign of friendship, *keeping secrets* seems like it would be the exact opposite. So by doing the opposite, by *not* telling Rachel that she used the phone, was Sofia showing herself indeed to be a true friend? I shake my head as I leave the barn. This strange behavior is most difficult to decipher.

Date and Time:

Wednesday, June 29, 2:50 p.m.

Location:

Camp Hollyhock, Redwood Shores, California

Description of Activity:

All the cabins are enjoying some free time after the hectic events of the Hollympics. Later this afternoon, we will gather in the barn for some crafting, but right now, I'm thankful to have the cabin all to myself to record my observations.

Reflections:

Another suspect—Subject Sofia—has arisen in the case of Subject Rachel's desecrated dog and pilfered phone, which, thankfully, continues to throw the blame off me. It's interesting that the two persons of interest are Subject Rachel's own friends. It's becoming clear that Subject Rachel is a terrible judge of character. I am going to have to reduce her Street Smarts score to a 3.

Since none of my cabinmates performed well in the Hollympics, their scores have not risen today. The exception is Subject Meg. Her archery skills could come in handy if we were stranded on a deserted island somewhere and needed to hunt animals for food. I will give her 2 more points in—

Excuse the interruption, but through our cabin's picture window, I have just witnessed a boy creeping around outside! It looks like Subject Quinn's boyfriend, Subject Jason. I must go investigate.

I push open the screen door at a glacial pace to prevent it from making its trademark squeak. After successfully exiting the cabin without a peep, I creep down the porch steps and take cover in the shade of a nearby maple tree to spy on the intruder. Jason is staring at one of our cabin's windows. The one that leads to Rachel's room. I whip around, grab a fallen branch nearby, and jog toward him, holding my weapon close to my side.

Jason turns at the sound of my footsteps.

"En garde!" I say, executing my best fencing flunge, a flying lunge. The tip of my saber-stick makes contact with his arm.

Jason nudges the stick away with his finger. "Didn't anyone ever tell you not to play with sticks?"

I whip my saber-stick through the air and, this time, aim it at his chest. "What are you doing sneaking around an all-girls camp?"

"I'm not sneaking anywhere," he says. "I came here from Camp Huckleberry with our camp director. Your camp borrowed some of our targets, and we've come to get them back."

"The archery supplies are by the barn, near the camp entrance. You're way off course."

He gives his head a shake to flip his hair out of his eyes. "Yeah, I was looking for the bathrooms. I guess I got lost."

I point my stick toward the path leading back to the main camp. "Bathrooms are that way." I point my stick back at his chest. "They're right by the barn. I'm not sure how you could have missed them."

Jason turns to look at the path and then at me. "Huh, I wonder how that happened." He makes no effort to leave.

I step closer to him, my saber centimeters from his solar plexus, the area just above his stomach. "Kindly remove yourself from the premises or I will be forced to alert camp authorities by screaming to the high heavens," I say.

Jason holds up his hands. "All right! Sheesh." He lopes over to the path. Before heading back to the barn, he flips his hair. "Will you tell Quinn I said hi?"

"No, I will not!" I shout, running in his direction to execute another flying lunge. "Now, get!"

He scrambles down the path. I jog after him to make sure he doesn't return. He picks up his pace, and I follow suit.

As we race down the trail, I hear a voice from above. "Hey, what's with all the running?" I stop and look up. Rachel is climbing down the limbs of an oak tree.

"I'm chasing Jason." I turn to look back at the path, but he's gone.

Rachel balances herself on the thick branch that's right next to my shoulder. "Quinn's Jason?" She takes a breath, then jumps to the ground. When she lands, she throws her hands up in the air like she's just completed a gymnastics vault. "I can't believe you'd chase after her man like that." She clucks her tongue against her teeth. "You *are* a little minx!"

My cheeks burn. "I'm not pursuing him romantically. He was lurking around our cabin staring at your window. If I hadn't stopped him, he might have tried to break in again."

"Again?" Rachel asks.

"He could have been the one who broke in to our cabin Monday night," I say. "He's certainly scrawny enough to squeeze through that little window. And he clearly knows how to sneak onto our campgrounds without being seen."

Rachel scratches her head. "Why would he steal my phone when he has his own?"

"That's a good point," I say. I slap the end of the stick on my palm. "Maybe he was borrowing someone else's phone, like Quinn was, and felt like he needed his own while he was at camp."

Rachel grabs the branch out of my hands. "How would he even know I hid my phone in a stuffed dog?"

I shrug. "Maybe Quinn told him?"

"Maybe." Rachel taps the end of my branch on the ground. "Maybe they were in on it together."

I shake my head. "I still don't think Quinn had anything to do with the murder and theft."

Rachel rolls her eyes. "Oh yeah, because her body language told you so."

I wag my finger. "Don't discount physical cues. The way someone uses their body when giving information offers vital clues about whether they are lying. Even the FBI—"

"Okay, okay, Abbyologist, spare me the lecture on the FBI." Rachel draws circles in the dirt with the stick. "What about Fia? Do you think she has it?"

I shake my head. "Consider the timing. Quinn says she borrowed the phone after Sofia used it to check World Cup scores. If Sofia had stolen the phone, Quinn wouldn't have found it when she snuck in to text Jason."

Rachel groans. "So now we're back to Quinn again."

"Or Jason." I take a step on the path toward the barn. "I wonder if I can catch him before he leaves camp."

Rachel moves in front of me to block my way. A silly grin rips across her face. "You certainly are interested in Jason."

I reach to grab my branch back. "I am only interested in talking to him about—"

She jerks away. "Oh, you want to talk to him, huh?" She walks around me, dragging the stick along the path.

"Yes, about what he was doing Monday night." My eyes follow her as she circles me.

"That's how it starts," she says. "First the talking, then the flirting, then the smooching." She starts making kissing noises.

"I would never kiss that boy." I grimace thinking of all the germs that could be running rampant in a twelve-year-old boy's mouth. "Or any boy, for that matter. The thought nauseates me."

Rachel stops and touches her chin. "What's that saying about the lady who protests too much?"

"It's 'The lady *doth protest* too much, *methinks*,'" I say, actually surprised she's heard of this quote from *Hamlet*.

Rachel's eyes twinkle as she raises her eyebrows.

"Oh," I say, understanding her meaning. Someone who denies something too intensely could actually be admitting their guilt. Classic Opposite Day Behavior. I drop my eyes to the ground. She's drawn a heart in the dirt with the stick. "I, under no circumstances, relish the thought of—" I stop, realizing if I go further, I'm falling into her trap again. I kick at the heart. "Will you just stop it?"

Rachel spins around and laughs.

"You have to know that you're being absolutely ridiculous, right?" I ask.

She pokes my boot with her stick. "I know. I know. I'm just doing it to bug you."

I cross my arms. "Why do you want to bug me?" I ask.

Rachel holds a pointer finger in the air. "*The idea nauseates me . . . under no circumstances . . . the correct term is . . .*" She giggles again. "Because I like it when you get that big-brained smartitude of yours. You puff up like my cat does when he's about to attack his favorite toy. It's adorable."

I crinkle my nose. "I am *not* adorable."

She points at me. "There it is. The adorable smartitude! You're a hoot and a half to hang out with."

"And that's a good thing?" I ask.

She swats a fly away. "Sure."

"So let me see if I understand this," I say. "You tease me because you enjoy hanging out with me?"

She shrugs. "Yeah, I guess you're growing on me."

Interesting. Rachel is verifying my theories about Opposite Day Behavior. She is warming to me and exhibits her feelings by insulting me. Could Opposite Day Behavior be a new theory about how teenage girls communicate with their own?

I should write a research paper on my ODB theories and present it to *Young Anthropologist*. Maybe they'll want to send me to the Eighth Annual Modern Anthropology Symposium to present my findings. The magazine reported that it was happening in Paris this year. Oh là là! The perfect title has just come to me: "Twelve-Year-Old Girls: *Comme Ci, Comme Ça*." Since the French saying *comme ci, comme ça* can be translated as both "so-so" or "like this, like that," the play on words is quite clever. This could be groundbreaking!

"Excuse me," I say, "but I really need to jot down some thoughts." I start jogging toward the cabin.

Rachel laughs. "Of course you do, Abbyologist!" she yells after me.

I bound down the path and up the porch steps. From the entrance, I can already see that something is wrong.

My mechanical pencil rests all alone on the table in the center of the common room.

"My field notes!" I shriek.

My journal is gone. I run across the room and look under the table, on the other chairs, even under the rug. Perhaps I put it back in my duffel before I confronted Jason. Doubt scratches at the back of my brain, but I search my room anyway, opening drawers and lifting pillows. I bend down to look under my bed. It's not there either. My chest tightens, as if a rope has wrapped itself around my lungs.

"Knock, knock," someone says from the front door. I walk back into the main room to see Emmy standing in the entrance. "Hey, there. It's time to head to the barn for crafting," she says.

"I can't go," I say "My journal's missing. My mother bought it on one of her business trips overseas. Its cover is made from genuine Italian leather. I have to find it."

"Oh, I'm sure it'll turn up," Emmy says, beckoning me toward the door. "Come on. We're making sit-upons. You don't want to miss that."

"I think someone stole it," I say, pacing the room.

Emmy clasps her hands behind her back. "That's a serious accusation, Abigail."

"Well, it's a serious crime, Emmy. I have important research in that journal."

Emmy walks toward me. "Who would want to steal your research?"

"Excellent question." I stop pacing. "Did you know I caught a boy sneaking around our cabin earlier?"

Emmy's pair of sandy blond braids sway as she nods. "I heard some of the Huckleberries were here getting some supplies."

I start circling the room again. "I bet that Jason kid snuck over here while I was talking to Rachel." I march to the table. "And then he broke in here and took my field notes." I pound my fist on the table. My pencil bounces. "Just like he broke in here the other night and took Rachel's ph—" I close my mouth, shocked that I almost just gave away Rachel's secret.

"Took Rachel's . . . uh . . . furry dog," I continue, pretending to pet Dabney with one hand, "and ripped its head off." With my other hand, I pantomime pulling off the dog's head.

Emmy blinks at me. "You think a boy from Camp Huckleberry broke into your cabin and destroyed Rachel's toy dog?" she asks.

I nod. "And stole my field notes."

"I think your notebook is going to turn up in this cabin somewhere, but right now we need to get to the barn." Emmy gestures me toward the door. "Hock-Eye is about to lead the sit-upon craft, and you know how she gets when Hollyhockers straggle in late."

Though Emmy is correct in pointing out that Hock-Eye hates tardy campers, she is completely off the mark about my journal. That Jason character is a thief, and I'm going to march into that barn and tell our camp director what he did. I follow Emmy out of Clovis Cabin and we head to the crafting event.

As Emmy and I enter the barn, we encounter a crowd of girls bunched around the Chore Chart, including members of Clovis Cabin.

"Hey, Hollyhockers! Keep it moving," Emmy says. "We can't get through."

"Look, Emmy!" Rachel points at a photograph on the bulletin board next to the listing of camp chores. The image shows Meg with her eyes squeezed shut. Her lips are touching some sort of creature she's holding in her hand. I squint to get a better look. It looks like a rotten banana. I gasp.

"Meg kissed a banana slug!" Rachel squeals.

I look at Meg in horror. Her round cheeks are flushed

pink, but the grin stretched across her face doesn't indicate she's the least bit embarrassed. She actually looks quite pleased with herself.

Emmy holds up a hand for a high five. "Nice job, Meg."

Meg smacks Emmy's palm with vigor. Emmy winces and shakes her hand.

"I can't believe you would do something so unsanitary," I say to Meg.

"I'd do anything for the Hollyhock Honor," Meg says. "It's no big deal." She shrugs. "They're actually kind of cute."

The girls grow rowdy as they crowd in on us, patting Meg on the back and offering congratulatory hoots. I feel myself start to sweat. I'm not sure if it's from the invasion of personal space or the thought of someone putting their mouth on a creature whose sole focus in life is to devour excrement.

I spy Quinn and Gabby sitting at a table with a pile of fabric at the center and stagger over to them.

"You okay, Abigail?" Gabby asks.

"Your outlook doesn't look so good," Quinn says.

I sink into the chair next to Gabby. "Did you know Meg kissed a banana slug?"

Gabby nods. "Yeah, I actually took that photo. I told her she was crazy, but she did it anyway."

"Excellent advice," I say. "Too bad she didn't follow it."

"Hey-ho, Hollyhockers!" Hock-Eye yells through her bullhorn. She stands on the stage at the front of the barn. Her frizzy gray hair poofs out around her aviators. Since she never takes those sunglasses off, I'm not sure how she's able to keep her "hock" eyes on us at all times.

"Hey-ho!" we yell back.

The girls at the Chore Chart disperse and scramble to their seats. Rachel, Meg, and Sofia join Quinn, Gabby, and me at our table. Hock-Eye shouts out instructions on how to sew together pieces of fabric and then fill them with stuffing to make sit upons. After her loud and thorough presentation, the girls start sorting through the pieces of fabric piled in the center of their tables. I stand from my chair to seek out Hock-Eye

"Hey, Abigail," Rachel says, pointing to the table next to us. "While you're up, will you see if the girls in Ponderosa Cabin have an extra pair of scissors?"

"You'll have to ask them yourself, I'm going to speak with Hock-Eye about Jason."

Quinn drops the pink and green bumblebee print she's holding. "*My* Jason?" she asks. "What about him?"

"*Your* Jason broke into our cabin today and stole my journal," I say.

Quinn laughs. "There is no way he would sneak into our cabin to steal your little diary."

"Pardon me," I say, crossing my arms. "But I do not write in a *little diary*. I record field notes in a research journal."

Quinn rolls her eyes. "Whatever. Jason wasn't even at Camp Hollyhock today." She returns to sorting through the fabric.

"Yes, he was," I say. "I saw him lurking around our cabin. He says hi, by the way."

"Oh, that's so sweet," Gabby says.

"You told me you caught him outside our cabin, not inside," Rachel says as she pulls a piece of white thread through a needle.

"What?" Quinn puts her hand on her chest. "You knew Jason was here and you didn't tell me?"

Rachel places her pointer finger on her chin. "Oh, did I fail to give you some important information, Quinn?" she asks in a high-pitched voice. Then she switches to a monotone: "My bad."

"Will you guys please turn it down a notch?" Meg asks. "Hock-Eye's coming."

"Oh good," I say. "I can speak to her about the break-in."

Quinn grabs my arm. "You will say nothing about Jason," she whispers.

"Or the you-know," Rachel says, making the phone sign and holding it to her ear.

"Clovis!" Hock-Eye barks as she looms over our table. "How's it going over here?"

"Awesome, Hock-Eye," Meg says, holding up her half-sewn sit-upon featuring a blue and gold anchor print.

"Marvelous work, Mary Elizabeth," Hock-Eye says. We can see the reflection of Meg's sit-upon in her sunglasses. "I particularly like how you chose a fabric in our camp colors." She fingers the edge. "And your stitching is just superb."

"Thank you," Meg says. Her smile is so wide I worry it might rip her cheeks open.

Hock-Eye marches over to me. She pulls her glasses down her nose. "Where's yours, Abigail?"

"I was just about to get started, but I needed to speak with you about something first."

Hock-Eye pushes her glasses back up and shakes her head. "We can talk after you make the sit-upon."

"But it's really quite important."

She picks through the leftover fabric on our table. "Right now, nothing's more important than your sit-upon." She pushes a large square of baby blue cotton with rainbows scattered all over it into my hands.

I can actually think of many things that are more important than sit-upons, like climate change, world hunger, and stolen field notes. But Hock-Eye has moved on to inspect Rachel's sit-upon. She picks it up and holds it between her fingers like it's a dirty diaper.

"You're supposed to begin sewing the fabric on the reverse side," she barks. "Then you flip it right side out to stuff it." She drops it in Rachel's lap. "You'll have to pull out those stitches and start over."

Rachel groans.

Hock-Eye pats her on the shoulder. "Carry on, Clovis," she booms before heading to the table next to us.

Since Hock-Eye refuses to speak to me about the break-in, I sit back down next to Gabby, and begin threading a needle.

"Sit-upons suck," Rachel says.

"Yeah, yours looks more like a frown-upon," Sofia says.

The table falls silent.

"JK!" Sofia says, then laughs.

No one responds.

Sofia stops giggling. "As in *just kidding*," she continues.

Gabby leans over and looks down the table at Rachel. "I think your fabric is amazing, Rachel. Don't give up!"

Rachel's mouth twitches into a small smile. "Thanks."

Sofia rolls her eyes, putting her whole body into it as she sweeps her head and neck up and down. "I think your fabric is amazing," she mimics.

"Leave Gabby alone," Rachel says. "She's being nice. You might want to try it sometime."

I watch the interchange wide-eyed. For some reason, Sofia's Opposite Day Behavior isn't having the usual effect on Rachel. Rachel's furrowed brow and angry tone indicate that she is genuinely displeased with the insults to her sewing.

Sofia's mouth drops open. "I told you it was a joke."

Rachel grunts. "Well, it wasn't funny. At all. Like most of your dumb jokes."

Sofia gasps, emitting a tiny squeak from her throat. She stands up from the table, pushing her chair back. "Sorry, but it's not my fault you have no sense of humor!" She grabs her sit-upon and then clomps away from the table.

I have a strong feeling that Sofia is no longer exhibiting ODB.

We all go back to quietly sewing.

After a few silent moments, Quinn addresses me. "So you're not going to say anything to Hock-Eye about Jason, right?"

I shake my head. "No, I'm still going to tell her." I hold up my sit-upon. "As soon as I'm done with this."

"But you have no proof it was him," Quinn says. "You can't go just go accusing someone of stealing without any proof."

"But Quinn, just a few days ago, you let Rachel make all those accusations against Abigail," Gabby says. "She didn't have any proof either. But now Abigail is in the wrong?" She shakes her head. "That doesn't make any sense."

"Actually, it does," I say. "Anthropologically speaking, it's natural for females to feel more kinship with the male they're mating with rather than other females of their species."

The girls all freeze and glance around at each other, smirking.

"Did you hear that, Quinn?" Rachel asks. "You're *mating* with Jason!" She puckers her lips to make kissing noises.

Gabby bursts out laughing, and the rest of the table joins in. All expect Quinn, who covers her face with her sit-upon.

"There's nothing to be embarrassed about," I say to Quinn. "Your feelings toward Jason are only instinctive."

The girls howl louder.

Rachel leans around Meg and holds up her hand to me. "Put her there, Abbyologist."

I slap her hand.

"Like I said, you're a hoot and a half," Rachel says.

Quinn hits our heads with her half-sewn sit-upon. "You guys, cut it out. I'm not mating with Jason, and you know it. He hasn't even asked to hold my hand yet."

"After two months?" Rachel asks, pushing stuffing into her sewn fabric squares.

Gabby sighs dreamily. "What a gentleman."

The girls snicker and giggle among themselves. Quinn focuses on her sewing and doesn't say anything more about Jason.

"Are you sure you didn't just misplace your journal?" Gabby asks me.

I shake my head as I tie a knot at the end of my thread. "I've already checked all the places I would have put it."

"So you searched the whole cabin, then?" she asks, pushing her needle through a green and blue pineapple printed fabric.

"Just my duffel bag, the common area, and our room," I reply.

"Don't you think you should look through the entire cabin first before you tell Hock-Eye about Jason?"

"Why would I have put it in someone else's room?" I ask.

"Maybe you didn't," she whispers. She places her sewing on the table and beckons me to come closer. I scoot my chair toward her. "I think we should search the entire cabin for your journal. Maybe we'll discover something else that went missing. If you know what I mean." She makes the universal sign for phone and holds it to her ear.

My eyes widen. I wonder why I had never thought of searching the cabin for the phone before now. "I do know what you mean. That is excellent advice," I say. "How do you propose we do it?"

"Tonight before lights out, you suggest that we all look through our rooms for the journal," Gabby says.

"But if I announce the search to everyone, the person who has stolen the journal and/or phone won't agree to it."

"Exactly," she says.

I gasp, breathless at her ingenuity. "Oh! The refusal will point to the real thief!"

Gabby nods. "Here's what you should do: First, tell Quinn you've decided not to report Jason. Then, later tonight . . ."

As she whispers her idea to me, I imagine we must look

like Jacqueline Richailbeaux and Mimi Le Goff do when they devise a scheme for trapping whatever smuggler, pirate, or tomb raider they've set their sights on. I also realize her hot breath on my ear isn't making me feel uncomfortable. I am actually allowing Gabby to invade my personal space! I do believe that my friendship experiment is just about complete. And this time, I predict the results will definitely be positive.

* * *

A few hours later, after sit-upons, dinner, and campfire songs, Meg, Rachel, and Gabby wrap up a card game they're playing at the table in Clovis Cabin. I stand in the center of the braided rug and cough to get their attention. "Excuse me, everyone. I have an announcement," I say.

Meg, Rachel, and Gabby put down their cards. Quinn appears at her bedroom door and stands in a tree pose. Sofia peeks her head out of the bathroom as she brushes her teeth.

"As you all know, my journal has gone missing," I say, carefully following the script that Gabby and I had prepared earlier today. "Originally, I thought that Jason had stolen it, but perhaps I was mistaken."

"Signs point to yes," Quinn says.

I look at Gabby, who nods at me with encouragement.

"The last time I saw the journal, it was in the cabin. So I propose that we search the entire cabin to look for it."

"That's actually a good idea," Rachel says.

I frown. That was supposed to be Gabby's line.

"I'm down," Sofia says through a mouthful of toothpaste.

"Me too," Meg says.

I look at Quinn. She nods deeply toward her hands, which are placed in prayer position in the center of her chest.

"This means we're going to search everywhere," I say, glancing from girl to girl, looking for some sort of negative reaction. "Every bedroom, every suitcase, every duffel bag."

Rachel stands from the table and claps her hands together once. "Let's do this."

Sofia emerges from the bathroom, wiping her mouth with the back of her hand. "Where do we start?" she asks.

Gabby stands and points at Rachel and Meg's bedroom. "Sofia, why don't you and Quinn search Meg and Rachel's room? Abigail and I will search yours. And Meg and Rachel, you guys will search ours."

My mouth drops open as I watch Rachel head toward my room. This was not part of the plan. "Wait a second,

Gabby," I say. "I've already looked through our room. It doesn't need to be searched again."

"Sometimes it helps to have a fresh pair of eyes look for you," she says.

I wave my hands in the air. "I don't like this one bit."

"But you're the one who suggested it," Meg says.

Sofia stops at the doorway to Meg's room and turns back to look at me. "You have something to hide?" she asks.

I freeze, realizing that the plan is inadvertently making me look guilty. "No, that's not it. I dislike people going through my things," I say, panic rising in my voice. "I have everything organized a certain way."

"Don't worry!" Rachel yells from inside my room. "I'll put everything back exactly the way I found it."

I question the likelihood of that happening. I watch the girls head toward their assignments. I'm amazed that not one of them objects to this search.

I sigh and enter Sofia and Quinn's room. Gabby has already opened a duffel bag. "You can go through that stuff over there." She waves her hand toward a suitcase in the corner.

I sit on the floor, looking at the case. The only thing worse than someone going through your dirty laundry is going through someone else's. I hold the zipper with the tips of my fingers and tug. I grab the flashlight from the desk and use it to push around the clothes inside.

"Darling PJs, Meg!" Sofia shouts from across the cabin.

"Seriously!" Gabby says. "How many pairs of black yoga pants does one girl need?"

"Abbyologist is the cutest!" Rachel yells. "She has days-of-the-week underpants."

Oh. The indignity.

Just as I'm about to explain the practicality of labeled undergarments, Rachel yells, "Seriously! I can't believe this."

I scramble up from the floor to see what has attracted her attention now. Gabby follows me. Rachel walks out into the main room, holding my field notes. The other girls emerge from the bedrooms and crowd around her.

I reach for my journal. "You found it! Where was it?"

With one hand, Rachel raises the book high in the air. Quinn grabs it.

"Wrapped up all nice and neat in your bathrobe, along with *this*," Rachel says. With her other hand, Rachel thrusts something in my face.

I have to back away to see what she's holding. It's a phone, with a giant crack across the screen.

The room erupts in gasps.

"Trouble ahead," says Quinn.

I gesture at the phone. "That's not mine."

"Duh." Rachel rolls her eyes. "Because it's *mine.*"

I rub the back of my neck, confused. "What would your phone be doing in my bathrobe?"

"Uh, maybe you stole it, broke it, and then hid it there?" Rachel says.

The girls stand in an assorted state of crossed-arms and hands-on-hips.

I am the accused. Again. This was not how this evening was supposed to turn out. My body stiffens. I shake my head. "Absolutely not."

Rachel enters my personal space and jabs her finger at me. "No wonder you didn't want us to search your stuff," she says. "You had this the whole time."

"I did not," I say, backing away from Rachel and into the table. "Whoever broke your phone hid it in my room. Obviously. Other people in this cabin have access to my belongings."

"So now you're accusing *me*?" Gabby stomps across the rug and glares at me over Rachel's shoulder. "The one person who's had your back?"

Her sharp words startle me. I shake my head. "No, I'm

just trying to make the point that anybody in this cabin could have infiltrated our room."

"Stop trying to confuse us with your fancy words, Abigail." Gabby wags her finger at me. "We may not be as smart as you, but we're not stupid."

I grip the edge of the table behind me. "Of course you're not stupid. I would never think that."

"Good," Gabby says. "Because I'm not buying your fake story anymore." She grabs Rachel's phone out of her hand and holds it up. "This proves you've been lying all along. I bet you even lied about being sick on Monday to use Rachel's phone for your field notes or whatever."

I shake my head. I must be hallucinating. The stress of the situation is causing me to imagine things. Surely my sweet roommate isn't acting like this. I squeeze my eyes shut, but when I open them again, Gabby is still there with her hardened eyes and defiant stance.

Gabby paces the rug, tapping the phone against her palm. "You probably meant to return it, but then broke it, panicked, and hid it."

"That does make sense," Rachel says, reaching out to grab her phone back.

Meg gasps next to me. "And then you made up that

phony story about how someone came in through our window," she says.

I turn to face her. "But *you're* the one who thought someone broke in. Remember how you freaked out, thinking you saw a face?"

Meg steps away and moves closer to Gabby, who's standing in front of the picture window. "You must have staged it somehow," Meg says.

My knees buckle. "What?" It feels like the room has tilted. "I did no such thing!"

"And *then*," Sofia says, joining Meg and Gabby at the window, "you try to pin it on Quinn's boyfriend."

"You probably made up the story about your journal being stolen too," Gabby says.

Sofia nods. "'Oh heavens to Betsy,'" she says in a high voice, clutching her cheeks with her hands. "My precious notes have been constipated." She drops her hands from her face and crosses her arms.

"The correct word is *confiscated*," I say. "And why would I steal my own journal?"

"To make it seem like you're not the real thief," Sofia says. "But to me it seems like a classic case of whoever smelt it dealt it."

"Whoever smelt it dealt it?" I repeat.

"You know, the first person who says they smell a fart is always the person who actually farted." Sofia shrugs. "You were the first to notice the journal was gone, so you must have been the one to steal it."

"But that doesn't make any sense. It's *my* journal. Of course I'd be the first to notice it's missing." I press my fingers to my temples. "All this nonsense is ridiculous. Someone is trying to trick you, Rachel. Can't you see that?"

Rachel bobs her head up and down. "Oh yeah, I can definitely tell when someone is trying to trick me."

"That's not what it says here," Quinn says.

I look up. She's leaning against the wall, flipping through my journal. "It says, 'Rachel is a terrible judge of character.'"

As I reach high for my field notes, my stomach feels like it's dropped to my toes. I have a strong feeling these girls aren't going to understand the anthropological aspects of my studies. "Please give that to me," I say. "It contains important research."

Quinn lifts the book higher in the air. "'I am going to have to reduce her smart score to a three,'" she reads.

"A three?" Rachel asks. "Out of what?"

I jump to grab the book, but Quinn jerks it toward the ceiling, still reading the open pages.

"That says *Street* Smarts," I say.

"Looks like she's measuring us on a scale of one to thirty," Quinn says.

"Three out of *thirty*?!" Rachel yells, stomping a foot.

"You don't understand." I bounce up and down, my arms thrashing in the air as I try to grab my field notes from Quinn. "It's a matrix based on three ratings."

"You're rating how smart we are?" Sofia asks.

"I got a three out of *thirty*!" Rachel repeats.

"What did I get?" Sofia asks.

"Looks like a four," Quinn says. Her mouth drops open as she slams the book closed. She glares at me. "You gave me a zero? Seriously?"

I'm finally able to wrench the book out of Quinn's hand. "How dare you go through my field notes!" My own piercing voice startles me. The book shakes in my trembling hand.

"How dare you give me a zero in intelligence!" Quinn says. "I got a ninety-eight percent in pre-algebra last year. Put *that* down in your little diary."

"It's *not* a diary!" I yell. I can't remember the last time I felt so angry. The sordid lies told about me. The violation of my private notes. The mockery of my research. I take a breath. "It's a journal." My voice quavers as I try to gain control of my emotions. "And I'm not evaluating intelligence."

"What are you evaluating, then?" Meg asks.

I clasp my journal to my chest. My heart pounds against it. "My research is confidential."

Sofia steps closer to me. "Not if it's about us." She reaches out to grab my field notes. "We have a right to know what's in there."

I turn away from her and grip the journal tighter. "If you must know," I say, "I'm researching friendship."

Rachel laughs, loud and hard. "That actually makes sense, because you, Abbyologist, do need to learn about that. You have no idea what being a friend means."

A surge of heat flushes across my cheeks. I drop my eyes to the ground.

There's a rap on the door.

Rachel shoves the phone down the waistband of her shorts, covering the top part of her phone with her T-shirt.

The door opens. Emmy steps inside. "Lights out in five minutes, campers!" she says.

"Got it!" Rachel answers.

Emmy looks around the room. Her eyes settle on me. She cocks her head to the side. "Is that your journal, Abigail? I thought you said someone stole it."

"Turns out she lied," Gabby says.

Emmy pushes back her shoulders. "Is this true, Abigail?" she asks.

"No," I croak.

But Sofia's words are louder. "It was in her duffel bag the whole time, along with—" Sofia suddenly stops as she sees Rachel make a quick slicing movement next to her throat.

"Along with what?" Emmy asks.

"Her days-of-the-week underpants," Rachel says quickly.

Emmy scratches her temple. "Okay."

"Who the heck wears days-of-the-week underpants?" Sofia's curls jiggle as she laughs.

Emmy ignores Sofia and walks over to me. "Do you have anything to say about this?" she asks me.

I have a lot to say. I want to shout about how I've been falsely accused of theft—again! How someone has gone through my unmentionables to plant evidence. How my private thoughts have been read aloud and taken out of context. How math proficiency has nothing to do with Street Smarts. How the one girl who I thought could be my friend is definitely not. How I'll probably leave camp just as I arrived—friendless. I swallow the anger and sadness that has thickened inside my throat and stand tall. "I have done absolutely nothing wrong," I say.

Emmy frowns. "Accusing someone of stealing is absolutely wrong," she says.

"Ha!" I scoff at the irony of her statement.

"This isn't funny, Abigail," Emmy says. "Do we need to get Hock-Eye involved?"

I nod. "Yes, I would love for Hock-Eye to hear about what's been going on in this cabin." I catch Rachel's eye.

Rachel jumps between Emmy and me. "No, no, no," she says. "No need to tell Hock-Eye. We can work out our problems among ourselves. Right, Abigail?"

I shrug and use this opportunity to employ one of Rachel's favorite expressions. "*What. Ever*," I say. "Now if you'll excuse me, I'm going to prepare for lights out."

Nobody says a word as I march into my bedroom. I lie down flat on my bed and stare at the mattress coils above me.

I hear Emmy talking to the girls in the main room. "Is everything okay with you guys?"

"Oh, we're fine," Rachel says. "I think we're all just a little tired. It's just been an overwhelming day. You know, with the Hollympics and everything."

"You guys better go right to sleep, then," Emmy says. "Tomorrow morning is the sunrise hike. We have to get up super early."

The girls groan.

"Happy Hollyhock dreams!" Emmy says.

After she leaves, the girls whisper together in the front room. Gabby stomps into our room and grabs her sleeping bag. "Meg and Rachel said I could bunk with them," she announces. "I don't want to share a room with someone who lies, steals, and spies on us."

I suck in my breath and turn to face the wall. I've never been physically hit before, but this must be what it feels like. I stare at the grooves in the cinder blocks and wait for Gabby to move her things. The others talk among themselves in the common area like I'm not here.

"I knew she was a weirdo when she started talking about room protocols."

"I could totally feel her bad energy."

"I can't believe she's never been sent to the principal's office before."

"She probably lied about that too."

After the last door closes, I roll out of bed and push my own door shut. The backs of my eyes prickle, and the room starts to blur. I bend down and grab the clothes piled outside my duffel and begin to fold them. A teardrop falls on my Friday underpants. I press the heels of my hands into my eyes and force myself not to cry.

I put on my pajamas, grab a flashlight and my journal, flick off the overhead light, and climb back into the bottom bunk. The full moon outside shines brightly through the small window, and the wind knocks the slightly crooked blinds. I lean against the wall and click my ballpoint pen. Another tear slides down my cheek. I'd like to blame it on some sort of allergic reaction, but the hard truth is I'm sad.

I wipe beneath my eyes and open my journal for probably the last time.

Date and Time:

Wednesday, June 29, 10:06 p.m.

Location:

Camp Hollyhock, Redwood Shores, California

Description of Activity:

Prowling, thieving, a frame job. You would think I had stumbled into a Jacqueline Richailbeaux movie, not summer camp. My undergarments were rifled through and so was my journal. I spoke angry words, gaped in speechless disbelief, and finally shed some tears. Yes, I am indeed crying as I record my last journal entry and put an end to this endeavor.

Reflections:

I really thought my experiment would be a success this time. I did everything right. I studied my subjects. I developed a mathematical formula. The numbers clearly pointed to Subject Gabby. Just a few hours ago, as she and I mulled over our foolproof plan, all signs indicated positive results.

But how could she fall for the elaborate plot that has been set against me? I'm going to have to reduce her score to—oh, silly me! Since the experiment is over, the scores are no longer needed. Which is just as well, as they turned out to be meaningless! How can Subject Gabby truly be my best friend? She should have believed that I had nothing to do with this ridiculous fiasco. But instead she turned on me. Viciously. She actually became one of my accusers and then called me a spy.

A spy uses her observations for nefarious results! I am not a *spy*. I am an *observer*. I am just trying to figure out which one of these girls would be a good friend. At least these results are conclusive: None of them are.

In fact, one camper here is determined to go to incredible lengths to prove that I'm a thief and a liar. Why? What is it about me that is so distasteful that someone would try to frame me for a crime I didn't commit? Is it my attire? Do I come off as a know-it-all? Are they jealous of my hula-hooping skills? What could it possibly be? This will just have to be one of the great, unanswered questions of our time, because Abigail Hensley is done with friendship experiments.

Now I understand why helium prefers to float all alone by itself. It's never had to experience the disappointment that comes with interacting with others. I'll be glad not to experience it again either. The false accusations and slanderous remarks. Silly nicknames and Opposite Day Behavior. Group hugs and high fives.

But now that I'm thinking of it, those weren't all that bad. And Subject Rachel and I had a few enjoyable moments together. And I like that she calls me Abbyologist. No one's ever given me a nickname that I actually liked before.

I apologize for the damp paper. These extra tears must be from fury because I can't understand why I would be so emotional about a girl who has limited street smarts, offers terrible advice, and interrupts constantly. Alas, the Sidekick Score is *morte*—dead. But there are certainly other reasons to be furious with Subject Rachel:

She continues to accuse me of criminal activity.

She hasn't figured out that the real person who stole and broke her precious phone is trying to draw attention away from herself and throw it on me.

She takes pleasure in annoying me and calling me adorable. Jacqueline Richailbeaux is never adorable! And a hoot and a half! Well, actually I don't mind that one so much. That must mean she finds me funny. No one has ever thought of me as witty. Oh dear, it seems the tears are never-ending.

Oh là là! Can it be? Am I actually becoming fond of this girl? Has she bewitched me with her Opposite Day Behavior? I should be angry with Subject Rachel, just like I am with Subject Gabby, but instead I'm depressed and confused. I have so many questions concerning Subject Rachel's conduct, but none of them are scientific.

Questions:

- Does Subject Rachel feel the least bit bad about my pitiful situation? Is she wondering about me? Will she ever call me a hoot and a half again?

Future Action:

Stop myself from succumbing to this ridiculous Opposite Day Behavior!

It is indeed always darkest before the dawn. Though the sun is set to rise in about twenty-five minutes time, we still need to use our flashlights to navigate the trail to the lake. Shadows from the trees creep across the narrow path as Emmy leads Clovis Cabin on our sunrise hike.

Nobody is alert enough to talk to one another or taunt me. The frogs are loud, though, arguing with one another over whatever frogs argue about. Lily pad privileges, which flies taste the best, who's the highest jumper. I smooth my hand down my arm, wiping away what feels like a spiderweb.

Suddenly, something tickles my back. I freeze. No one should be behind me, since I am the caboose of our little trekking train. I flip around anyway to see if one of the girls snuck back there and put something down my shirt, but the path is empty.

As soon as I turn back around to the front, I feel it again. I squeak and do a little jig, jumping up and down and shaking my shoulders, hoping to dislodge whatever night creature has decided to attach itself to me. I hop, stomp, shake, and wiggle until I'm finally satisfied my back is bug-free. I find myself alone on the trail, as the other girls have carried on without me. I pick up my pace to catch up with them. My flashlight's beam bounces across the ground as I start to jog.

All at once, the frogs stop croaking. I stop to listen for whatever has caused their sudden silence. Some leaves rustle, but there is no wind this morning. I point my beam into the tree above me. It's probably just a squirrel jumping through the branches. But then the rustling grows louder and louder. It sounds like it's coming from my right, just off the hiking path. I shine my light into the darkness. The rustling stops. Just then, I see a shadowy two-legged figure moving through the trees. Perhaps Meg was right. Maybe there really are ax-murdering lumberjacks wandering through these woods!

I turn to run, but I trip on a tree root and come crashing to the ground. My flashlight bangs against a rock and rolls off the path toward the figure, just like in a horror movie. I scramble to get up and start running.

Without my flashlight, I can't see much. I head straight into a bush of some sort. Prickly branches scratch at my arms and legs. I retreat and wipe more spiderwebs from my arms. My scared heart seems to have jumped for cover inside my head. Every heartbeat feels like it's banging against my skull. I swing my body wildly around. Where is everybody?

The rustling stops. I freeze. And then the frogs pick up their croaking right where they left off. I can't hear a thing over the noise. I take a careful step forward and then another. I look down, focusing on the rocky ground to make sure I stay on the path. This might be the way to the lake. Feeling more confident, I walk faster.

Suddenly I ram right into something again. "Oof," the something says, grabbing my arm.

I struggle to pull my arm away. "Unhand me this instant, or I'll scream," I say. "My counselor is just up the path."

The something flashes a light in my face. "Abbyologist, it's just me!"

I blink into the brightness. The something is Rachel. She releases my arm while I'm in mid-jerk, and I stumble backward.

"Okay, you've had your fun scaring me halfway to Hades," I say. "What are you going to do now? Tell the girls I was so frightened I peed in my days-of-the-week underpants?"

"Oh my God, did you?" She hands me the flashlight I dropped.

"Of course not, but I'm sure Sofia would love that detail." I grab the light.

Rachel giggles. "Yeah, she probably would."

I stomp past her. I can hear her boots tramping behind me.

"Why aren't you with the others?" I ask.

"I came back to talk to you," she says. "Sorry if I scared you."

"What do we possibly have to talk about?" I ask.

"It's about my phone," she says.

I stop and turn around to face her. Rachel almost slams right into me again. I aim the beam of my flashlight into her face.

"Don't you dare try to tell me I need to replace that broken phone of yours!" I shout. "I don't care if that phone was found in my robe. I never touched it, used it, broke it, or stole it. And I refuse to—"

Rachel holds up her hand to shadow her eyes from the beam. "Relax," she says. "I know."

"You know *what*?"

"I know it wasn't you."

"Oh," I say, surprised. "Well . . . good." I turn and continue walking down the path. "I'm glad that's settled."

"Me too," Rachel says as she follows behind me.

I turn back around and flash my light on her again. "If you knew it wasn't me, why didn't you say something last night?" I ask. "Why did you allow the girls to continue to believe I did it? They all hate me now."

Rachel shines her light in my face. "Why did you give me a smart score of three?"

I drop my beam and eyes to the ground. "Quinn read it wrong. It was Street Smarts, and it doesn't matter anyway. That matrix has an error."

"Street Smarts?" Rachel repeats. "What the heck does that even mean?"

"It's your ability to think quickly, exercise sound judgment—"

Rachel plants a hand on her hip. She shifts the beam of her flashlight. Her face has flared into a simmering glower.

"Never mind," I say. "Like I said, that matrix doesn't work. It's all wrong." I head toward the lake again.

"You bet it's wrong," Rachel says as she stomps next to me. "Because last night as everything was going down, I used my *sound judgment* to *quickly think* to myself: Something about this story doesn't sound right. I just couldn't buy that it was you who staged the break-in or pretended to steal your own journal."

As we tramp down the path together, the beams from our flashlights skip along the ground in front of us. "Obviously," I say. "Even if I did steal your phone and my journal—which I didn't—I wouldn't be foolish enough to hide them together. Thank you for realizing I'm smarter than that."

Rachel shakes her head. "It has nothing to do with how smart you are. It actually has to do with mean kids."

"Mean kids?"

"I may not be as smart as you about foreign movies, grammar, and archeology, or whatever ology you're into, but I do know kids."

I nod as I listen. Rachel's right. She is probably more of an expert in this particular field of study.

"Some kids can play mean and dirty," she continues. "Some kids would lie, steal, and blame other kids to get out of paying for a broken phone and getting in trouble with Hock-Eye. Those are the mean kids. And, even though I'm super mad about what you wrote about me, I can tell that deep down, you are not mean."

I turn to Rachel. "No, I'm not."

She looks at me. We lock eyes for a moment and then return our gazes to the path in front of us. Our boots crunch the dried leaves in tandem.

"And there was something else that bothered me about what went down last night," she says.

"What?"

"Not a what, but a who: Gabby. Did you see the way she turned on you? She's been sugary sweet to you—to all of us—this whole time. I saw how the two of you were so chummy making sit-upons last night. Then *bam!*" She claps her hands together. The frogs stop croaking. "She starts accusing you, shrieking like a crow. Why do you think she'd do that?"

I kick a stick off the trail. "Because she's not my friend."

Rachel snorts. "Yeah, definitely not. In fact, I bet you a brand-new phone she's the one who broke mine and then framed you for it."

"Gabby?" I shake my head. "I don't know. She doesn't seem like a mean kid either."

"Think about it," Rachel says. "She's your roommate and can easily get to your stuff. And remember, she's the one that told me and Meg to search your room? She knew we would find the phone because she put it there."

I suck in a breath as I realize Gabby is the one who came up with the whole search idea to begin with.

"I'm telling you, Gabby's a mean kid," Rachel says.

"She's more than mean, she's diabolical," I say. "Kudos to you for seeing through her scheme."

"Not bad for a girl who's a terrible judge of character and has a Street Smarts score of three, huh?"

I wince as she throws my words back at me. "I'm so sorry. I should never have written those words down. Not only are they hurtful, but they're wrong. If I were still using the matrix, I would increase your Street Smarts score to an eight."

"An eight?" Rachel says, giving me a playful shove. "I deserve a ten!"

"Perhaps," I say, shoving her back. "But, as I've said, the matrix is flawed."

"Uh, yeah," Rachel says. "Street smarts have nothing to do with friendship."

I nod. "You are correct. Proof being that Gabby scored high in this area."

"See, there you go," Rachel says. "After this is all over, I should really give you some pointers on how to make friends. Matrix and journal not required."

"I think I might like that," I say. "My methods are clearly not working. But when will this all be over?"

"When I get Gabby to confess that she broke my phone," Rachel says. The sky has started to turn purple. Rachel starts walking faster. "Come on, we're going to miss the sunrise."

"How are you going to get Gabby to confess?" I ask.

As we trot briskly down the trail, she explains that she doesn't want Gabby to know she's figured out who really broke her phone. Instead, Rachel plans to make Gabby her new best friend to get close to her. She doesn't think it will take her long to get my roommate to slip up and expose her crime.

"I know how to play dirty and mean too," she says.

"Gardez vos amis près et vos ennemis loin," I say.

"English, please," she says.

"It means you're keeping your enemy close," I explain. "You'd make an excellent secret agent."

The trees that line the path start to thin, the sound of water trickling along the shore grows louder, as do the sounds of the girls' giggles.

"Does that mean you're cool with all this?" Rachel whispers as the lake comes into view. It shimmers in the growing morning light. "You're going to have to pretend that you really did steal the phone, so Gabby doesn't know that we suspect her. Can you do that?"

"I don't like the idea of taking the blame for something I didn't do," I say.

"Think of it as payback for all those mean things you wrote about me," she says.

I sigh. "This scheme reminds me of Jacqueline Richailbeaux pretending to be a deranged psychic in *The Lost Phantom*."

"O . . . *kay*. Does that mean you're in?"

"I have always wanted to engage in a game of subterfuge," I say.

"I'll take that as Abbyologist for *yes*," she says.

We step onto the wooden pier and take in the sunrise. The rest of Clovis Cabin sits at the very end, their shadowy backs to us. Golden rays peek through the trees surrounding the lake. The water sparkles around us. It really is a spectacular sunrise.

"Okay," Rachel says. "The plan starts now. We can't let the girls see us together, so wait here for a bit before you follow me down."

I nod and watch her head toward the end of the pier.

"Later, *frien-amis*," Rachel says, walking away.

I smile at her unsuccessful attempt to roll her *r* like a true Parisian and her clever wordplay that includes both the French and English words for friends. But wait. Perhaps she actually is calling me her *frenemy*, a word that often comes up in my research on teenaged behavior. According to Merriam-Webster's Online Dictionary, a frenemy is one who pretends to be a friend but is actually an enemy.

Is Rachel using Opposite Day Behavior again? Are we indeed friends? Or are we enemies? Are we both? Or neither? I shake my head as I make my way to the end of the pier. I will never understand that girl's behavior.

* * *

After the sunrise hike, we return to Clovis Cabin. As the last camper to enter the cabin, I close the front door and lean against it. "I have an announcement," I say.

The girls stop talking and glare at me.

"I will be brief," I say, pressing a closed fist to my chest. "This morning during the hike, in my darkest of darkest hours, I realized I could not tell a lie any longer." I close my eyes and take a breath for dramatic effect. "I stand before you this morning, confessing to my crime. I did indeed . . ." My throat closes up. The words don't want to come out. I am physically struggling with this lie.

"You did indeed what?" Rachel prompts, sounding annoyed.

I clear my throat. "I did indeed break your phone, Rachel. I wanted to borrow it for my field notes, but I accidentally dropped it."

"Uh, tell us something we don't know," Sofia says.

Meg tugs at a pigtail. "Why are you confessing this now?"

"I cannot hide from the truth any longer," I say. "I promise to replace the phone after camp is over."

Rachel walks over to Gabby and hugs her tightly. "Thank you so, so much," she says. "Because you told us to search Abigail's room, we finally got her to fess up." The girls finish hugging, but Rachel keeps an arm firmly planted on Gabby's shoulder.

"Oh my gosh." Gabby's eyebrows creep up her forehead as she turns to face me. Her eyes catch mine for a brief moment before they dart back to Rachel. "You're super welcome."

"Unbelievable," Quinn says. She uncurls herself from a butterfly pose on the table, jumps down, and stands next to Sofia and Meg. "I can't believe how much good energy was blown trying to figure this whole thing out, and it was you all along."

"Yeah, like that stupid trial you put us through," Sofia says. "What a waste."

"Actually, that was your idea," I say.

"And we have to continue rooming with the Big Fat Liar," Sofia continues. "That's not fair."

"Outlook grim," Quinn says.

"Hold on," Gabby says. "Sofia, you and Quinn both lied to Rachel about using her phone. Remember?"

Quinn whispers into her cootie catcher while Sofia inspects her fingernails.

Interesting how Gabby is taking my side again. Now that the blame has been firmly attached to me, she can go back to being her sweet self. I narrow my eyes at her. Only Rachel and I know the real truth.

"My point is, we've all made mistakes," Gabby continues. "So I say we give Abigail a break."

I really want to stare daggers into her lying eyes, but instead I hang my head in shame.

"I hope this means this whole phone business is finally over," Meg says.

I nod solemnly.

"And this better not happen again," Meg continues. "No more lying, right?"

I clear my throat in preparation for another big performance. "You do not have to worry. I will not be stealing or lying anymore. Pinky promise." I walk over to Meg and hold up my pinky, but she just glares at it. I curl the little finger back down into my fist and pound my chest for dramatic flair. "I am really, really sorry for causing all this terrible, terrible trouble. I have learned my lesson. Yes, sirree, I have."

"And so have we," Rachel says. "Right, girls?"

"Right," they all say together.

"We'll be keeping our eyes on you," Rachel says. She walks toward me and puts her face just inches from mine. She points two fingers to her eyes and then at mine. She whips around, and her hair slaps me in the face. I have to spit some of it out of my open mouth. Time to brush my teeth again.

If I didn't know any better, I would be convinced Rachel hated me too.

Date and Time:

Friday, July 1, 12:07 p.m.

Location:

Camp Hollyhock, Redwood Shores, California

Description of Activity:

Contrary to what I wrote in my previous entry, I have decided not to abandon my experiment entirely. Since Subject Rachel has agreed to give me some guidance on how to make friends, I've resolved to give it another go but without the Sidekick Score. However, things are on hold while she tries to unmask Subject Gabby's deception. Subject Rachel must pretend that she still believes I broke her phone and that Subject Gabby is her new best friend, so it would be inappropriate for us to fraternize.

Subject Rachel deserves an Oscar for her performance. Subject Rachel laughs at everything Subject Gabby says, braids her hair, and offers fashion advice. They eat together, canoe together, and hike together.

This charade hasn't been as interesting as I had originally thought. I haven't been given much opportunity to show off my acting skills. I don't have to pretend how unpleasant it is to be disliked and ignored.

Most of the subjects follow Subject Rachel's lead and ignore me completely. However, there has been one surprising development. Subject Meg has broken from the pack. She says because I've proven myself to be such a great camper, she doesn't care so much about the phone business. She's even written me a meaty role in the script she's writing for Hollyhock's Hollywood Night.

Tonight each cabin will act out a skit on the barn stage after dinner. We're determined to put on the best skit Camp Hollyhock has ever seen! That is, Subject Meg is determined. The campers performing in the winning skit receive extra points for the Hollyhock Honor. Subject Meg is not only writing the script, but also directing the whole thing. Rehearsals begin in the barn this afternoon.

Reflections:

I do wonder whether Subject Meg is exhibiting Opposite Day Behavior and is really showing her dislike for me. Previous observations indicate that Subject Meg is unfamiliar with ODB, so she *could* genuinely like me. But I have not forgotten that Subject Gabby acted similarly, so I remain wary. After the events of the past few days, it's difficult to know whether I can truly trust anyone. I worry whether I will ever be able to make a real connection with a girl my age, which saddens me.

I'm also troubled by the fuss Subject Gabby makes over Subject Rachel. I can't deny how annoying it is to hear my roommate go on about her new BFF. "Rachel did the funniest thing. Rachel has the best hair. Well, Rachel says . . ." Rachel. Rachel. Rachel. I think Subject Gabby should feel a tad guilty since she knows I'm taking the blame for something she did. Could she be a budding psychopath?

Another interesting development in the cabin is Subject Sofia. You would think Subject Sofia would have something to say about the way Subject Gabby fawns all over Subject Rachel. But Subject Sofia has not uttered one disparaging word. For once I find this disappointing, considering how obnoxious Subject Gabby is being. In addition, Subject Sofia's "jokes" have stopped and so have most of her insults. She's hardly said a word these past couple of days. If the Sidekick Score were still functional, she would have a 10 in Quiet Listening skills.

I suspect the reason behind Subject Sofia's behavior is that she's confused by Subject Rachel becoming so close to someone who is sweet and kind, and not snide and snarky. She's realizing that perhaps her cutting jokes and comments aren't doing her any favors, especially when it comes to her friendship with Subject Rachel. Since she doesn't really know how to act, she just keeps quiet.

Question:

- Will Subject Meg turn out to be an appropriate friend for me? She had the second-highest rating in the immensely inaccurate, now defunct Sidekick Score. Thus, another reason to be wary of her.

Future Action:

Wait patiently for this ruse to finish so that Subject Rachel can properly advise me on how to make friends.

Rachel, Quinn, Sofia, and Gabby stand in their designated places on the stage. Meg and I watch from the wings. For the past two hours, we've been practicing our skit. Appropriately enough, it's a murder mystery based on the classic board game Clue.

Quinn plays the glamorous Miss Scarlett and Meg the fuddy-duddy Mrs. Peacock. Sofia is the grumpy billionaire, Mr. Green, and Gabby the mousy chambermaid, Mrs. White. My role is that of Professor Plum, of course. Meg has chosen Rachel to play the dimwitted Colonel Mustard. It has become quite clear during this afternoon's rehearsal that Rachel has been miscast.

The part of Colonel Mustard is a comedic role that includes a silly Southern accent, funny one-liners, and some slapstick. Unfortunately, it turns out that Rachel has no comedic timing. She stutters through her punch lines, refuses to do the pratfalls, and delivers her twang as if she's sucking on a marble. In addition, Rachel can't remember any of her lines.

"Fwankly mah deah, Mizz Scahlott, Ah don't give a dern," Rachel says.

"Cut!" Meg screams, pushing herself through the side curtains and stomping out to center stage. "Seriously, Rachel? Again?"

"Hey!" Rachel shouts. "I know I said that one right."

"You did," Gabby says, "and it was so super funny." Gabby holds her stomach like she's containing a belly laugh.

Sofia opens her mouth as if to say something but then snaps it shut.

"It's just that you're supposed to say it in the next scene," Gabby continues. She walks across the stage to show Rachel her script. "See?"

Rachel grabs the paper from Gabby and groans. "Why do I have so many words to say?"

"It's not that hard to memorize a few lines." Meg smirks. "The rest of us managed to do it."

"Are you calling me stupid?" Rachel asks.

Sofia opens her mouth again but says nothing and bites her lip instead.

"You said it," Meg says. "Not me."

Rachel lunges toward Meg. Gabby steps between them. "Oh my gosh, Rachel, you are *so* not stupid." Gabby leads Rachel back to her place in the center of the stage. "You'll get it this time. Quinn, say your line again."

Quinn straightens up from a chair pose she's been

squatting in at stage right and says, "I do declare that it was Professor Plum in the billiard room with the rope."

Rachel opens her mouth, scratches the back of her head, then throws down the script. "This play sucks." She storms off the stage and down the half dozen steps that lead to the floor. "I quit."

"Wait." Gabby chases after Rachel and grabs her arm before she can head out of the barn. "Don't go. It won't be the same without you. I can help you memorize your lines."

"I don't need any help—especially from you." Rachel jerks her arm away with such force that she accidentally shoves Gabby into the wall and the bulletin board next to the door. The board crashes to the ground.

Gabby's face crumples as she watches Rachel leave the barn.

Meg claps her hands. "All right, people," she says. "Sofia, you'll have to take over as Colonel Mustard." Meg looks down at her script and sighs. "You guys take five while I rework some lines and figure out what to do with Mr. Green."

I decide to use this time for a secret rendezvous with Rachel. Since she and Gabby have been inseparable, I haven't had a chance to talk with her alone and find out what she's gleaned from this false friendship. I head toward the exit, passing Gabby as she hangs the bulletin board back on the wall. The right corner of the board tilts down. As I reach over to straighten it, Gabby sniffs. "I just don't understand why she's so rude to me," she says.

I push up the bottom corner of the bulletin board so it lines up squarely on the wall. Rachel really needs to do a better job of controlling her emotions. If she's not careful, she will expose the ruse.

"I mean, I'm so nice to her," Gabby continues. "I offer to help her. I pump her up. I'm the only one that tells her she's doing great as Colonel Mustard, and still, she talks to me like that."

I chew on my lip for a few moments, unsure how to respond to her. I certainly can't explain the real reason behind Rachel's anger. I decide to give a different explanation. An anthropological one.

"That's how Rachel shows she likes you," I say. Some of the photographs and papers that were pinned on the board have scattered on the floor. I bend to pick them up.

Gabby squats next to me and collects some fallen pushpins. "By pushing me and yelling at me? That doesn't make any sense."

"Consider this. Quinn, Sofia, and Rachel are good friends. Think about how they act sometimes." I stand and hold a photograph up to the board. "They insult each other, call each other stupid, tell each other to shut up," I explain. "They all think it's hilarious."

Gabby stands up straighter and hands me a pin. "Yeah, I guess."

I push the tack into the photograph and attach it to the board. "So the way Rachel just acted toward you was just her way of expressing her friendship. She even told me—when we were on better terms, of course—that she expresses affection by picking on her friends."

Gabby doesn't say anything for a few moments. Perhaps she's feeling guilty for befriending Rachel while Rachel and I are no longer on good terms.

I take the pushpins from her and continue replacing the photographs.

Gabby sucks in a breath. "Abigail?" she starts.

"Yes," I say. Is this it? Is this the confession we've been waiting for? Can we finally be done with this charade?

"Thanks for helping me put this back." She turns and heads toward the stage.

I sigh. It's just as well. I would need a corroborating witness to the confession anyway. Otherwise it would just be my word against hers. Again.

With the bulletin board put back together, I continue

on my way to find Rachel. I survey the campgrounds, wondering where Rachel could be. According to any episode of every kid-com that airs on the Family Network, when girls get upset, they run to their rooms and throw themselves facedown on their beds. I beeline to our cabin and open our front door. Just as I expected, the door to Rachel's room is closed. I knock softly. There's no answer from the other side, so I open the door.

"Did I say you could come in?" Rachel says. She tosses a pillow at me from the top bunk and flops over on her bed.

"You didn't say I *couldn't* come in," I reply.

"Can you leave?" she says.

"I was hoping we could have a private tête-à-tête." I reach down to grab the pillow.

"Whatever that means, I'm not up for it," Rachel says. "I'm in the middle of a pity party."

"Oh, okay." I walk the pillow over to her. "Let me know when it's done."

As she turns to grab it, I notice her splotchy face and red, watery eyes. I think she might be crying. The last time I found myself alone with a tearful girl was during the fairy wand incident. Dashing out the front door and waiting on the curb for Mom to come rescue me is probably not the appropriate response here.

I climb the ladder to the top bunk and perch on the edge of the bed. "Do you want to talk about it?" This seems to be the common remedy for tears on the Family Network.

"No!" She puts the pillow over her face.

I take a deep breath. I had hoped it wouldn't come to this. "Do you need a hug?"

Rachel lifts up the pillow and peeks out. "Seriously? You want to hug it out right now?"

"Not especially," I say. "But I will. For you." These words surprise me. But they are true, which is also mildly shocking.

A smile creeps across Rachel's face. She tosses off the pillow, sits up, throws her arms around me, and squeezes tight.

"Is this making you feel better?" I ask. I must be getting used to this hugging business. Despite my face being pinned against her shoulder, I don't feel as uncomfortable as I usually do.

"Not especially," Rachel answers. "I just wanted to see you all squirmy."

I find myself actually wanting to put my own arm around her and start to lift it, but the squeezing stops. I freeze. "Are we finished?" I ask.

She releases me and throws herself back on her bed. "Do you think I'm stupid?" she asks.

"No, not at all," I say. "The whole plan of yours to trap Gabby was actually quite clever. I'm surprised I didn't think of it myself."

Rachel sniffs.

"You don't seem convinced," I say.

Rachel shakes her head. "Meg's right. I should be able to memorize a few lines, but I can't."

"Of course you can," I say. "You just have to use a few memory tricks. I can teach you some if you'd like."

Rachel flops around and looks at the wall again. "They won't work. I've tried that before. My memory is broken."

"A broken memory? I've never heard of such a thing."

"Trust me, it's a thing," she mumbles. "Just ask my doctors."

"Are you talking about your working memory?" I ask. "Do you have trouble remembering new information?"

Rachel flips her head back around. "How do you know about working memory?" she asks.

"I read about it in a parenting magazine."

Rachel laughs. "You read *parenting* magazines?"

"I read everything. And don't try to change the subject." I wag my finger at her.

She buries herself under the pillow again and moans.

"That's why you couldn't remember the order of your

lines," I say, slapping my hand on the bedsheets. "And why your sit-upon was sewn incorrectly. You have trouble remembering certain details, which makes it hard for you to follow directions."

Rachel says nothing for a few moments. Then the pillow moves slowly up and down like she's nodding.

"And this makes you feel stupid?" I ask.

Again, the pillow nods.

"Well," I say, "you'll be happy to know that according to *Caring Parent*, working memory problems have absolutely nothing to do with your intelligence. You are not dumb. And that's a scientific fact."

Rachel emerges from the pillow again, a small smile creeping across her lips. "Thanks, Abbyologist. But what I really want to know is whether I have a perfect ten in Street Smarts."

I groan. "You'll never let that go, will you?"

Rachel shakes her head. "Nope."

I grab the pillow from her and swat her gently. "Fine, you've got a ten. Happy?"

"Very." She pulls herself into a sitting position. "Now what is it that you want to do? Something about a tutu?"

"A tête-à-tête is a conversation," I explain. "Have you learned anything from Gabby? Any chance she confessed?"

Rachel shakes her head. "I haven't been able to get anything out of her. Either she's a really good liar or she had nothing to do with busting my phone."

"Hmm," I murmur as I rub the back of my neck. "Have you looked at your phone to see if she left any clues?"

She cocks her head. "What do you mean?"

"Did she text anyone, like Quinn did, or watch a video, like Sofia? She must have used it for something before she broke it, right?"

"I didn't see any texts," Rachel says. She jumps out of her bunk. "But I didn't think about searching the browser history." She pulls the phone out of her duffel bag.

I climb down the ladder and stand next to her.

Rachel turns on the device and swipes her finger across the cracked screen. She taps it a few times. "Nope, nothing here, except for the sports website Sofia used."

I remember the pictures that were spread across the barn floor moments ago. "Any photos?" I ask.

She shakes her head. "No photos either."

"If she did take any photos, she probably deleted them," I say. "She wouldn't be foolish enough to leave them for you to find."

"But . . ." Rachel says as she swipes and taps. "I have this app that retrieves deleted stuff."

"Are you girls using an electronic device?" someone says from the direction of the bedroom doorway.

Rachel shrieks. I turn toward the voice. It's Hock-Eye.

"That is a direct violation of Section Three, Article Two of the Hollyhock Handbook." She thrusts her palm out. "Hand it over, girls."

Date and Time:

Friday, July 1, 5:36 p.m.

Location:

Camp Hollyhock, Redwood Shores, California

Description of Activity:

My worst nightmare has become reality. I've been cleaning restrooms all afternoon. Upon seeing that all the bathrooms have lidless toilets, I had to manufacture my own hazmat suit out of black plastic garbage bags and three pairs of rubber gloves. Upon seeing my suit, Rachel said I was a "hoot and two halves" until I gravely told her that toilet water can erupt up to twenty feet out of the bowl when flushed. I advised that she should wear one too. She did not argue.

Reflections:

This punishment that Subject Rachel and I are suffering through is most unwarranted. We are both victims, her phone having been violated and me being falsely accused.

Subject Rachel tried to explain to Hock-Eye that we were using the phone to solve a crime. She told Hock-Eye that there is a thief creeping around camp who broke Subject Rachel's phone and stole my field notes, but Hock-Eye wouldn't listen to our reasoning. "Rachel brought an electronic device to camp!" she barked. "And you were both caught using it."

During her reprimand, the toilet in Laguna Cabin overflowed, sending six girls squealing across the campgrounds and Hock-Eye into the supply shed banging around for a plunger.

After getting the plumbing situation under control, Hock-Eye suspended Subject Rachel and me from camp activities for the rest of the afternoon and ordered us to clean up the mess in Laguna Cabin, followed by the rest of the bathrooms at Camp Hollyhock. In addition, we cannot participate in Hollywood Night and are deemed ineligible to receive the Hollyhock Honor. This award will be presented tomorrow night in the barn during the Holly-Huck Hoedown, the coed social event between Camps Hollyhock and Huckleberry that marks the end of our week at camp.

Perhaps these consequences would be easier to endure if we indeed were able to access the deleted photos on Subject Rachel's phone.

Questions:

- How are we going to see the photos now that the phone is locked in Hock-Eye's cabin? Can we prove that Subject Gabby broke the phone before camp ends tomorrow?

Future Action:

Mess duty. Camp-speak for cleaning up the kitchen.

"Honestly," I say, scouring crusty tomato sauce off a kitchen counter. "Why did tonight have to be chili night?" Whoever was on food duty made a concentrated effort to use every pot, utensil, and dish on hand and spill on every available surface.

"Hock-Eye probably planned it." Rachel attacks an iron pot with a wad of steel wool. "To punish us extra hard."

Raucous hoots erupt in the barn.

"Sounds like Meg's skit is a hit," I say.

"The person who busted up my phone should be out here slumming in all this muck," Rachel says, slamming the pot into the sink. "It kills me that we're not going to be able to prove Gabby did it."

"Maybe we still can," I say. "I've been trying to figure out how we can get to the phone in Hock-Eye's cabin. It involves a clever distraction à la *Jacqueline Richailbeaux and the Sunken Skull*. However, I'm not sure if the camp has any gunpowder or firecrackers on hand."

"Uh, probably not. But we don't need any of that," Rachel says, her face brightening. "Hock-Eye is already distracted."

She walks over to the door that looks out into the barn. "By Hollywood Night."

"I suppose that could count as a distraction." I frown. "But I was hoping for something more clever and dramatic."

Rachel pulls off her rubber gloves and throws them on the counter. "There are at least three other groups that need to perform their skits. That should give us plenty of time to get my phone back." She starts heading out of the kitchen.

Before she can leave, I grab her arm. "You mean right now?" I ask. "We don't even have a plan."

"What's to plan?" Rachel says. "We just break into her cabin and find the phone."

"But we don't have a key."

"The cabin windows are old, and most of them don't lock anymore. I'm sure we'll find a way in." She tries to pull away from me.

I pull her closer. "What if Hollywood Night ends earlier than we thought and Hock-Eye heads back to her cabin while we're still in there?"

"Good point." Rachel tries to pry my fingers off her arm. "For someone who has personal space issues, you sure are invading mine pretty harshly right now."

I suddenly notice that Rachel's face is just inches from

mine. How did that happen? I release my grip and take a step back.

"You stay here," Rachel continues. "Keep an eye out. If you need to, come up with a clever and dramatic distraction. One that doesn't involve fire."

"What about the kitchen?" I ask. "We're not finished."

"Something for you to do while you're keeping an eye out," she says. "Now, I've gotta go, or we'll definitely get caught." She steals out of the kitchen and tiptoes toward the barn's main exit.

I don't need Quinn's cootie catcher to sense that trouble is indeed ahead. I finish scrubbing down the kitchen, keeping one eye on the barn exit. As I'm placing dishes in the old wooden cabinets, I feel a sting in the back of my hand. I pull my hand out and notice a splinter of wood has lodged near my knuckle. I try to pull it out, but I only push it in deeper. I fuss with it some more, becoming so preoccupied I almost don't notice Hock-Eye barreling out of the barn. Curses! I forgot to come up with a clever distraction!

I follow her outside. "Hock-Eye!" I shout.

She aims her flashlight at me. "Yes?"

"Um. Where are you going?" I ask.

"To grab a sweater from my cabin."

"No!" I yell.

"Excuse me?"

"I mean 'Oh!' As in, 'Oh, that's interesting.'" If Jacqueline Richailbeaux were a real person, she would be disgusted with my diversion skills.

"I didn't know my choice in clothes was so fascinating to you girls," she says as she continues waddling toward her cabin.

"Wait, Hock-Eye!" I yell again. "Come see how clean the kitchen is."

"I'm sure it's fine, dearie."

"Please, come look." I sweep my arm back toward the barn. "I want to make sure we did a good job. I'd hate to disappoint you. Again."

Hock-Eye sighs. "All right. But make it quick. It's getting chilly out here."

We walk back inside the barn and to the kitchen at the rear of the building. I cover my ears as one of the girls sings an off-key rendition of "On Top of Spaghetti." Hock-Eye gives the kitchen a cursory glance. She doesn't even remove her sunglasses. "Just as I thought. It looks great." She turns to leave.

"Wait." I grab her arm and pull her back in. "What's your opinion on these canned vegetables over here? I think they should be organized by color, but then perhaps alphabetical order makes more sense."

"I don't think the vegetables need organizing," Hock-Eye replies. "Why don't you go enjoy the last few minutes of Hollywood Night? I think you and Rachel have learned your lesson today." She surveys the kitchen again. "Where is she, anyway?"

"Oh. Uh . . . uh . . . she went . . ." I bite my lip hard, hoping to jump-start my brain. It works. Finally! A coherent thought. "She went to the bathroom."

"When she comes back," Hock-Eye says, "please tell her I thought you both did a great job."

"Okay." I give her a salute. "Will do."

I watch, frozen in place, as she heads toward the cabins again. I'd never thought I'd ever experience this in all my life. But my mind is blank! Not literally, of course, due to this unhelpful nonsense currently running through it right now. Figuratively, it is empty. I circle the kitchen, trying to think of something. I rub the spot on my hand that stings from the splinter. I glance down. That's it!

I race out of the barn and down the trail leading to the cabins. I catch her just as she's walking up the steps to her cabin. "Hock-Eye!" I yell.

"What is it now?" she asks.

"I have a splinter." I show her my hand. "What should I do?" As the words come out, I cringe, hating how foolish I sound. Everybody knows what to do with a splinter. Pull it out!

Hock-Eye puts my hand underneath the beam of her flashlight. She even lifts up her sunglasses to get a good look. "Oh, that's a bad one," she says, perching her glasses in her nest of frizzy gray hair. She turns and puts her hand on the doorknob. "Come inside. I have some tweezers in the bathroom."

"Okay, Hock-Eye!" I yell, hoping to warn Rachel that we're entering the cabin and to hide—quickly. "I'll come inside with you to get some tweezers from the *bathroom!*"

Hock-Eye frowns at me. "No need to yell. I may be old, but I'm not deaf."

"Sorry. I don't know what's wrong with me. Maybe the pain is affecting my brain," I say. I push past her as she opens the door.

The hum of air-conditioning greets us. Hock-Eye turns on the light. To the right of the front door is a desk, where a laptop sits. Hock-Eye grabs a brown cardigan from her desk chair and tugs it on. She pulls a phone out of the pocket and swipes at the screen. The Hollyhock rule about electronic devices obviously doesn't apply to everyone.

Something bangs from across the room. It sounds like it's coming from the closed door in the corner of the cabin.

Hock-Eye looks up from her phone. "What was that?" she asks.

"What was what?" I say. "I didn't hear any noise at all."

Hock-Eye starts walking toward the closed door. I move in front of her, blocking her path, and hold up my hand. "We really should do something about my splinter before it gets infected," I say.

The doorknob turns. I squeeze my eyes closed. Whatever happens next, I can't bear to watch.

"Oh, hello, dear, I forgot you were here," Hock-Eye says. "Did you find what you were looking for?"

I open my eyes. Emmy is exiting the bathroom, holding a bottle of antacid tablets.

"Yes, thanks," she says. She puts a hand on her stomach. "Chili and I do not get along."

"Would you please help Abigail with her splinter?" Hock-Eye asks. She waves her hand toward the bathroom. "There should be some tweezers in there."

"Sure thing," she says.

Where in the world is Rachel? I glance around the main room. In addition to a desk, there's a threadbare green sofa and a wooden coffee table covered with papers. Something shiny glimmers at the table's edge. I do a double take. It's Rachel's phone.

Emmy gently takes my hand. "Ouch," she says. "That looks like a nasty one."

Hock-Eye walks to the front door. Before she heads back into the night, she says, "Please remember to lock up before you leave."

Emmy holds up a set of keys and jingles it. "Will do," she says.

The front door slams shut. The cabin shakes, and the door across from the bathroom creaks as it opens wider. Rachel must be hiding in the darkened room.

"Oh, the agony," I say, as I push Emmy into the bathroom. "It really hurts." Once we're both inside, I close the door behind us.

"Okay, just give me a minute," Emmy says as she turns and opens the medicine cabinet above the sink. The mirror on the cabinet's door reflects the interior of the bathtub.

I draw in a breath. Rachel! In the angled mirror, I can see her hiding behind the partially opened shower curtain. I let out a squeak like a kitten that's just had its tail stepped on.

"Don't cry," Emmy says as she rummages through the cupboard. "I'm really good at first aid."

Rachel holds a finger to her lips and carefully steps deeper into the tub, concealing herself further behind the curtain, rippling the fabric.

Emmy slams the cabinet door shut and turns to look at the shower curtain. "What the heck?"

I grab her arm and pull her attention back to me. "Please hurry, Emmy," I say. "According to the FunWithGerms website, if a splinter isn't removed quickly, it can become infected, cause tetanus, and in some instances, death."

"Relax, Abigail," Emmy says. She notices the open bathroom window next to the shower. "Ugh, look at all these bugs getting in. Hock-Eye really needs to keep these windows closed or the mosquitoes are going eat her alive." She pulls the window closed.

I stare at the back of my hand, feeling nauseated, but not about impending gangrene. It's the looming possibility of Rachel getting discovered at any moment!

"Tweezers aren't here," Emmy says. "Gotta go see if we have any in the supply shed. I'll be right back." Emmy opens the bathroom door.

I watch her leave the cabin. Rachel climbs out of the tub.

"You were supposed to *dis*tract, not *at*tract!" Rachel says.

"What are you doing in here?" I ask. "The bathroom is the very last place I would search for a phone."

"I didn't even get a chance to look for it." She points at the window. "This was the only window that ended up being unlocked. And then, just as I finished crawling through it, I heard the front door open. I barely had time to hide in the tub." She heads out of the bathroom. "We better look for the phone fast before she comes back."

I point toward the coffee table. "It's over there. Hurry!" I stand by the window to keep an eye out for Emmy.

Rachel jogs across the room and picks up the device. She swipes the screen and presses one of the icons. She nods. "Oh yeah. Gabby, you are so busted." Her eyes widen. "Wait. These photos aren't of Gabby."

She walks over to me and shows me her phone. The screen shows Meg blowing a kiss to the camera. At the bottom of the image, the word *busted* has been scrawled with a photo app. Rachel swipes her phone. There's Meg wagging her finger at the camera. This time, the message at the bottom reads: *payback*. Rachel swipes again. A third image appears, this one of Meg sticking her tongue out and holding her plaid water bottle. Wait. That last picture isn't Meg.

We look at each other. Now we know for sure who broke Rachel's phone.

* * *

About fifteen minutes later, Rachel and I collapse into two chairs in Clovis Cabin's common room. I press my hand against my pounding heart and take a few deep breaths. Tears stream down Rachel's cheeks. She's been laughing herself silly.

"This is you when you saw me hiding behind that shower curtain," Rachel says. She drops her mouth open, raises her eyebrows dramatically, rolls her eyes back into her head, and makes a squeaking noise.

"You scared me halfway to Hades!" I say.

"*Halfway to Hades!*" Rachel repeats, laughing even harder.

"I was sure we were going to get caught," I explain. "Actually, it's amazing that we didn't. How did you not run into Emmy on your way out? I swear she came back with those tweezers mere seconds after you left."

"I know. It was pretty close," she says. "I had to sneak behind a tree. And she must have heard me too, because she shined her flashlight all around my hiding place. But then

you made that yelping noise, and she ran inside the cabin. That was a clever and dramatic distraction, by the way."

I hold up my bandaged hand. "You're quite welcome."

The door to Clovis Cabin swings open, and the other girls tumble inside.

Meg runs circles around the room, pumping her fist in the air. "We killed it!" she says. "You're looking at the winners of this summer's best skit."

"'Without a doubt,'" Quinn says, tucking her cootie catcher into her back pocket.

"Did you hear everyone cheering for us?" Sofia asks no one in particular. "I'm definitely going out for the drama team this fall."

"You mean *club*," Meg says. "Acting is not a sport."

"Sorry you missed it, Rachel." Gabby throws me a quick look. "Oh, and you too, Abigail."

"Way to go, Meg!" Rachel yells. "With your four bull's-eyes in archery, your stunning sit-upon, and now your award-winning skit, you should definitely win the Hollyhock Honor tomorrow night."

"You think?" Meg bounds onto the table, holds up her flashlight, and shakes it in the air, as if it's a major award she has just won. The rest of the girls surround the table and clap for her. I join in. Rachel whistles.

Meg pretends as if she's giving an acceptance speech. "Thank you so much for this amazing honor. I wouldn't be here tonight if it wasn't for the great wisdom of my sister." The girls of Clovis Cabin laugh and clap some more.

As the applause quiets, Rachel continues to clap loud and hard. "Speaking of your sister," she says. "What do you think she'd say about campers who violate the Hollyhock Handbook? Would she say they deserve to win?"

Meg points her nose to the ceiling and shakes her head. "No. That's why it's such a crime that you won last year, you know, because you snuck in your phone."

Rachel taps her chin. "Interesting," she says. "She'd probably say you don't deserve it either."

Meg crinkles her forehead. "I didn't bring a phone to camp."

"That's true," Rachel says. "But you did steal mine. That's even worse."

Meg's face grows pink. "I did no such thing," she says, then jumps off the table.

Sofia politely raises her hand like we're in school. "Uh, why are we talking about Rachel's phone again? Abigail already told us *she* broke it."

"That's right," Meg says, standing as tall as she can.

"You confessed, Abigail." She glares at me. "You can't take it back now."

"Oh, just shut it, Meg!" Rachel says. "I saw the photos of you on my phone."

Meg's eyes widen. "But that's—"

"Impossible?" Rachel smirks, walking toward Meg. "I have an app that tracks my deleted stuff. So, yeah, you're the one who's busted!" Rachel steps into Meg's personal space. "You've known all along Abbyologist didn't really break my phone. That's why you've been so buddy-buddy with her the last few days. Guilty much?"

Aha! My suspicions were correct. Meg was indeed exercising Opposite Day Behavior by being kind to me. And how clever of her to pretend she was clueless about ODB to throw me off! It's *Opposite* Opposite Day Behavior.

"Okay, hold on," Quinn says. She closes her eyes, touches her thumbs and pointer fingers together, and takes a deep breath. She opens her eyes. "Are you now saying Abigail *didn't* steal and break the phone?"

I shake my head. "I gave what is called a false confession," I say. "In most cases, people give them to protect a family member or loved one. But in this instance, it was a ruse. Rachel thought Gabby was the real culprit."

Gabby throws her hand to her chest. "Me?" she squeaks.

I ignore her outburst. "Rachel hoped if she became BFFs with her, Gabby would eventually tell her the truth," I explain.

Gabby moves her hand to her hip and glares at Rachel. "All this time you were pretending to be my friend?"

Rachel takes a defensive step backward, even though Gabby hasn't moved an inch toward her. "No offense," Rachel begins, "but come on, Gabby, you do plenty of pretending too."

"What are you talking about?" she asks, now with both hands on her hips.

"*Oh my God, that cootie catcher is so awesome, Quinn,*" Rachel says in a falsetto.

"*Rachel, it's just so amazing that you've been to Japan,*" Sofia adds, rolling her eyes. "You can't expect us to believe you mean all that," she says in her normal voice. "We're not idiots."

"Well, excuse me for being nice," Gabby says.

"There's a difference between being nice and being fake," Quinn says.

Gabby stomps her foot. "I am not fake!" she yells.

I clear my throat. "I don't think that Gabby means you any harm by saying those things. She just wants to be your friend."

"Then just be your true self," Quinn says. "Like you're being right now."

"Yeah, I like this Gabby," Sofia says, pointing a pink fingernail at her. "She's real and edgy. She tells it like it is. She has a spine."

The corner of Gabby's frown twitches as if she's about to smile. "Since we're being real," she says. "Quinn, Jason is too short for you. Rachel, it was a stupid idea to bring your phone to camp. Meg, tell her that you broke it and that you'll replace it so we can be finally done with this."

I blink at Gabby. Her bluntness is still surprising.

"It might not be as simple as that," I explain. "There was one last photo—"

"Fine!" Meg yells. "It was me!"

I now find myself blinking at Meg. "What did you say?" I ask.

Meg looks down at the floor. "You heard me. I stole it. I took those pictures."

"Why?" Rachel asks.

Meg sighs. "I was going to threaten to turn you in if you didn't help me win the Hollyhock Honor," she says in a small voice.

"Ohhh," Rachel says. "So that's why you scribbled

payback on that selfie." She suddenly gasps, as if in shock. "You were going to blackmail me?"

If I were the eye-rolling type, I would be doing so at this moment. Not too long ago, Rachel was using the same tactic on me.

Meg nods, kicking at the floor.

"But you never said a word to me," Rachel continues. "Why?"

Meg shrugs. "Things just got all screwed up when it broke."

"How did the phone break?" I ask.

Meg shrugs. "Does it matter how? It was an accident."

"But you're admitting that you did it?" I ask.

Meg sighs. She doesn't say anything for a few moments, and then finally nods.

"And you'll replace it?" Rachel asks.

Meg closes her eyes and nods again. When she opens them, they shine with tears. "Just please, please promise me you won't tell Hock-Eye. I don't want to lose my chance at winning the Hollyhock Honor. My sister will kill me if I don't come home with one."

Rachel looks at Meg for a long time. Nobody makes a sound. I count the seconds to myself. After the eleventh Mississippi, Rachel finally speaks. "Okay, I won't tell."

Meg drops into a chair.

"Wow, Rach," Sofia says. "That is super nice of you." She throws a glance toward Gabby. "And I totally mean that."

"Without a doubt," Quinn says.

Rachel shrugs. "It's like Meg said. I violated the Hollyhock Handbook last year and still won. If I tattled, I would be a hippocrust."

"I believe the word you are looking for is 'hypocrite,'" I explain, "where your actual behavior doesn't match the moral standards you claim to have."

"Hold on a second," Gabby says, "Shouldn't you have a say in this, Abigail? You were a victim too." She stomps across the rug to stand in front of the chair where Meg sits. She wags her finger at her. "You stole her journal and then planted the phone inside it to make it seem like she stole it."

Meg opens her mouth to speak, but then bites down on her lip.

Sofia joins Gabby. "You were going to let Abigail pay hundreds of dollars to replace something she didn't break," she adds.

Meg looks up at the girls and then over at me. A tear slides down her cheek. "I'm so sorry," she whispers. "I was afraid I'd get in trouble and get sent home from camp.

My sister would never let me live that down." She hugs herself. "You don't know what it's like living with Miss Perfection." She holds a hand up to her forehead and snuffles behind it.

We all watch her shake on the chair and exchange glances.

Rachel bends forward to catch my eye. "What do you say, Abbyologist? I'm getting a new phone. Your name is finally cleared. Can we finally let this drama go?"

"Signs point to no," Quinn says.

I should be outraged how Meg's shenanigans have affected my camp experiment. But instead of anger, I feel pity. Someone else is involved in this scheme. There's proof on Rachel's phone. But for some reason, Meg is taking all the blame. I walk over to Meg and reach my arm out to her. How does this work? Do I rub her back? Pat her head? Unfortunately, I think a little more is necessary here. I bend down next to the bunk and make a semicircle with my arms.

Gabby grabs my wrist and pulls me up. "Really?" she says. "You're going to give *her* a hug?"

"Isn't this what you're supposed to do when someone is sad?" I ask. "Show them compassion?"

"She doesn't deserve it," Gabby snaps. "She broke the phone, lied about it, and let you take the blame."

"No thanks to you," I remind her.

Gabby shifts her gaze away from me and grabs one of her red curls to twirl between her fingers.

"And obviously, Meg feels bad about it now," I say.

Meg moves her head up and down, still hiding behind her hands.

"She only feels bad because she got caught," Quinn says.

Meg shakes her head. "That's not true," she says, emerging from behind her fingers. "I feel terrible about what happened, Abigail. You turned out to be a really good camper. You didn't deserve any of this. I'm so sorry."

I squat back down next to Meg. "I can see that," I say. "I will keep the secret if that's really what you want."

Meg freezes as if she's thinking about it one last time, and then nods.

I reach out again to Meg, and this time, decide to pat her.

"Ow." Meg grabs her upper arm with her hand.

"Too hard?" I ask.

She nods her tear-stained face but offers me a meager smile.

"Sorry." I decide not to give the patting another try, and stand. "And I forgive you for allowing me to take the fall. After all, self-preservation is a natural anthropological urge."

"Thank you." Meg sniffs, wiping her nose with her sleeve.

"But because of her, we thought you were a liar," Sofia says. "And a thief."

"We were kind of awful to you, Abigail," Gabby says, looking at the ground.

I raise my eyebrows. Kind of?

"Sorry about that, by the way." Quinn fiddles with her cootie catcher. "That wasn't cool of us."

I hug my elbows. No one's ever apologized for being rude to me before. "It's okay," I say. "I probably would have done the same if the situation were reversed. Herd mentality can be quite a strong impulse."

"You cleaned the bathrooms and kitchen all day," Gabby says. She throws her hands up. "You missed Hollywood Night!"

"True. But if I would have gone to Hollywood Night, I would have missed out on some especially thrilling fieldwork."

"What were you doing in the field during Hollywood Night?" Sofia asks.

"I think she's talking about how we snuck into Hock-

Eye's cabin tonight to get one last look at the phone," Rachel says with a grin. "That's how we found the photos of Meg."

Gabby puts her hands on her cheeks.

"Un. Believe. Able," Sofia says. "You broke into Hock-Eye's cabin?"

"Technically, Rachel did the breaking and entering," I explain.

"And Abbyologist did the freaking outing," Rachel says, tilting her head toward me. "You should have seen her. She looked like she was going to pee her days-of-the-week panties."

I sigh. "Must we bring those up again?"

"Did you get caught?" Gabby asks.

Rachel shakes her head and says, "But we *almost* did, like a zillion times—"

"I believe the more accurate number is three," I add.

"And the best part was when Abigail got a splinter, which created a clever and dramatic distraction." Rachel holds up my injured hand.

Sofia reaches over and swats me on the arm. "Way to take one for the team, Abigail," she says.

"Thanks, friend," Rachel says as she grips my hand, careful not to squeeze my injury.

I stiffen. My eyes widen.

Rachel must notice my reaction because she drops my hand and steps back. "Oh yeah, personal space. Sorry."

I shake my head. "It's not that." I point at her. "You called me *friend*."

She scrunches up her forehead. "Uh, yeah?" she says.

I nod. "Was that a mistake in terminology?"

Rachel scratches her chin. "There's something about you, Abbyologist. I don't know. Those things you wrote in your journal really hurt my feelings, but when you and I weren't speaking for a couple of days, I kind of missed you."

I nod in understanding. "I enjoy your company too, which is odd, because according to the data I've collected, you and I are absolutely not compatible."

"That proves it, then," Rachel says. "We're meant to be friends!"

I squint at her. "I'm not following your reasoning."

"You said yourself that your vortex, mortax, or whatever you call it, was screwed up," she explains. "So if it proved that we're *not* supposed to be friends, then the opposite is true."

I slowly nod my head. "That actually makes sense," I say. Perhaps my matrix is salvageable after all, but in the true spirit of Opposite Day Behavior, the results come out reversed.

"I can't believe I'm saying this, but you're right. We are indeed friends," I say, holding out my hand.

Rachel looks down at it. "What are we doing here?"

"Making our friendship official."

"By shaking hands?"

"How else do we do it?" I ask.

"I'll give you a hint," Rachel says. She flashes her evil grin and opens her arms.

"Oh no," I say.

"Oh yes." Rachel grabs me close.

"Group hug!" Sofia yells.

I hold my breath and squeeze my eyes shut in anticipation of the crush of bodies.

The girls shriek and howl with laughter. We jump up and down on the rug for a few moments before toppling into a huge heap. One by one, the girls roll away, giggling about the events of the last week. All except Meg, who's still slumped in her chair looking miserable.

Rachel clambers up from the rug and holds out a hand to pull me off the rug. I look at Meg. "What are we going to do about her?" I whisper.

Rachel shrugs. "Nothing. She's admitted to breaking the phone. We didn't force her. She'll get her Hollyhock Honor, I'll get a new phone. It's a win-win."

"But we both know Emmy was in that final photograph," I say. "I think Meg knows it too."

The other girls call out "Happy Hollyhock dreams!" as they cross the cabin from bathroom to bedroom and start preparing for bed.

Rachel sighs. "There's nothing we can do about it now. Just forget about it." She heads into her bedroom.

I wish I could. But the solution to the problem is completely wrong. Somehow, Rachel and I have to get Meg to show everyone the right answer before camp ends.

Date and Time:

Saturday July 2, 8:14 p.m.

Location:

Camp Hollyhock, Redwood Shores, California

Description of Activity:

The whole of Hollyhock and Huckleberry are huddled up in our camp's barn for the Holly-Huck Hoedown. Contrary to what its name suggests, this social occasion has nothing to do with gardening tools. From what I can gather, this event involves the boys and girls from both camps standing along the perimeter of the barn, staring blankly at one another. Some of the girls dance among themselves to the blaring music. Subjects Sofia, Rachel, and Gabby are cutting a mean rug in the middle of the barn, as are other girls from the Eureka and Ponderosa cabins.

As of yet, I have witnessed no mingling among the genders, not even between Subject Quinn and Subject Jason. For someone who was so desperate to see Subject Quinn the other day, he seems to be working really hard to not even glance her way now. Instead, he seems to find the snack table quite interesting, especially the trail mix, which he has been throwing at his buddies, despite Hock-Eye's continued reprimands. I wonder if Subject Quinn will even care if Hock-Eye throws Subject Jason out of the hoedown. The last time I saw her, she was sequestered in a corner with some girls from Laguna Cabin, dishing out fortunes with her cootie catcher.

Every few minutes or so, Subject Rachel bounds over to my chair and tries to pull me onto the dance floor. I politely decline. My graceful fencing maneuvers do not translate well into dance moves. And besides, I want to use these last few moments of camp to gather my final thoughts.

Reflections:

I must admit the results of my Camp Hollyhock experiment were quite surprising. Especially because I had hypothesized that Subject Rach and I could never be friends. But sometimes in scientific experiments, proving a hypothesis to be wrong can also mean success. And that indeed is the case here.

There is another surprising result from this experiment: Subject Rach lives in a town just twenty minutes away from mine, so we will have ample opportunity to strengthen our friendship. We have already scheduled a sleepover for next weekend at my house. I plan to show her my favorite movie: *Jacqueline Richailbeaux and the Man from Moldavia* and serve my favorite meal, croque monsieurs. I also wanted to have a pillow fight, but Subject Rach said no one actually has pillow fights at slumber parties. She suggested makeovers instead and promises to use only toxic-free cosmetics.

We've spent so much time planning our slumber party that we only had a few minutes to discuss the Meg situation. Why is she covering for Emmy? There's no doubt she's been a supportive and helpful counselor, but I can't imagine why Subject Meg would feel the need to protect her. Subject Rach told me not to worry—that everything will work out the way it's supposed to. She pinky promises.

I wait until the snack table is clear of Huckleberries and walk over to grab a drink. While sipping punch, I notice Quinn sitting on a chair in butterfly pose, her hands folded in prayer at her chest. I head her way and sit in the folding chair beside her.

"This seems like a weird time to be doing yoga," I say.

"There's nothing weird about the practice," she says with her eyes closed. After a few seconds, she groans and opens her eyes. "I can't focus."

"The music is pretty loud in here."

"It's the bad energy," she says, staring at Jason. He and another Huckleberry swat each other with their baseball caps.

"Are you and Jason in a fight?" I ask.

She looks at me as if I have just asked her if he has alien tendencies. "My reply is no. Why would you think that?"

"I admit, I am not an expert in this particular area of study," I say. "But aren't girlfriends and boyfriends supposed to talk to each other at these types of social gatherings?"

"My sources say yes, but . . ." She stares off into space.

"But?" I ask.

She leans toward me. "I don't want to talk to him," she whispers. "I don't even *like* him."

It seems that Opposite Day Behavior even applies to the opposite sex. "I see. You don't like Jason, so you agreed to be his girlfriend?"

Quinn shrugs. "It's not like I hate him or anything. It's just . . . a lot of the girls at school are getting boyfriends now, and in the crowd I hang out with, it's kind of expected that I should have one too. Jason was the first one to ask me to go out, and I said okay without thinking too much about it. Now I wish I hadn't. Secretly texting him wasn't worth the trouble it caused with Rachel. And, oh my God." She points at him. "Just look at him."

We both spend a few moments watching Jason pretend like he's going to vomit on a gaggle of girls from the Goldenstar Cabin. He jerks, heaves, and clutches his stomach. As he opens his mouth and stumbles, the girls squeal and scatter.

Quinn shakes her head. "He's no Alex Michaels."

"Who's that?" I ask, before taking another sip of punch.

"This adorable boy at my school." She holds up her cootie catcher. "We're going to get married."

"Why don't you ask him to be your boyfriend?"

She shoves me. "Are you nuts? I can't do that."

"Why not?" I ask, checking to make sure none of the red juice sloshed onto my shorts.

"What if he says no?" she asks.

"What if he says yes?" I ask back.

She smiles.

"From recent experience," I say, "I've learned that sometimes if you do the exact opposite of what you think you should do, you will produce the results you want."

"Hmm," Quinn murmurs. "Highly doubtful." She holds up her cootie catcher. "Let's ask the Coot." She closes her eyes and whispers to it: "Should I ask Alex to be my boyfriend?"

She swishes the paper back and forth between her fingers five times, than twelve, then another five. After three final swishes, she hands me the contraption. "Here, you tell me what it says." She points to the flap of paper I'm supposed to read.

I lift up the flap and read: "'My sources say yes.'" I show her the words. "See, even the Coot agrees."

Quinn makes a little squealing noise, unfolds herself from her pose, and heads toward Jason.

"Please, let him down easy," I tell her.

Just as Quinn begins her trek across the barn to break

Jason's heart, Hock-Eye yells through her bullhorn that the Huckleberry and Hollyhock Honors are about to be announced. I get up from my chair and start hunting for Meg. I'm interested to see what happens if she indeed wins, as we suspect she will.

The crowd begins slowly moving toward the stage at the front of the barn. I keep my eyes peeled for the inhabitants of Clovis Cabin. I see Rachel up onstage. As last year's winner, she is charged with presenting tonight's award. She waves at me and points toward the left side of the stage. I head in that direction and find Meg and Emmy standing together whispering, their dirty blond braids sway together as they lean into each other. I stop for a moment. I consider their matching braids, their tiny frames, their fair features. I remember how I first thought that last photograph on Rachel's phone was Meg because she was holding a plaid water bottle with the monogram *M E G. M . . . E . . .* I suck in a breath as I finally realize why Meg is covering for Emmy. They're *sisters*.

Meg sees me and steps away from Emmy.

Emmy turns around. Her furrowed brow relaxes a little when she sees me.

"Hey, Abigail," Emmy says. She gestures to Sofia and Gabby who look slightly moist as they gulp down some water near the snack tables. "There's the rest of your crew over there."

"Yes, I see," I say. "I just wanted to wish Meg good luck. I hope you win, Meg."

"You do?" they both say at the same time. They both scrunch up their eyebrows.

"Of course," I say. "Meg has proven herself to be the best camper here, and she totally deserves it."

"That's so nice of you to say, Abigail," Emmy says.

"Yeah, uh, thanks," Meg says. She looks like she's going to throw up.

"Hey-ho, Hollyhockers and Huckleberries!" Hock-Eye's voice booms through her bullhorn.

"Hey-ho!" Everyone chants back.

"It's now time for the distribution of the Hollyhock Honor. Here to present this year's award is last year's winner, Rachel Lin."

Rachel steps up to a microphone. She hits it a couple of times. "Is this thing on?" she asks. The mic screeches an answer. Rachel giggles and reads from a piece of paper. "I get to present the Hollyhock Honor to a crazy cool camper. She is a superior scavenger and an amazing archer. She created a great God's-eye and super sit-upon. And she wrote, directed, and starred in a superb skit last night!"

Emmy nudges Meg. "That's you! You're going to win!"

Meg scratches at her elbow.

"This hecka amazing Hollyhocker is loyal and dedicated to her fellow campers." Rachel moves her eyes away from the paper and over to Meg. "She is honest and always follows the rules of the Hollyhock Handbook. And," she says slowly, "she always does the *honorable* thing. This year's Hollyhock Honor goes to Mary Elizabeth George, or, as we all know her, Meg!"

The Hollyhockers and Huckleberries clap for Meg. Emmy shakes her fist in the air and yells, "Woo-hoo!"

Meg sighs and shuffles to the stairs leading to the stage. She doesn't look very happy.

I lean toward Emmy and whisper, "We know it was you who broke Rachel's phone, Madeline Elise."

She swings around to look at me. "If I were you, I'd keep my mouth shut," Emmy says. "You don't know what you're talking about."

I nod. "Didn't Meg tell you? The photos that were deleted on Rachel's phone were recovered. We saw the selfie of you. It was the last one."

"So what?" she says. "That doesn't mean I broke it."

The mic screeches again. Emmy and I look up at the stage. Meg is accepting a bouquet of Hollyhock flowers from Rachel. Meg looks out at the crowd, shielding her eyes from the spotlight shining in her face. She clears her throat. "I am honored to be chosen for this, um, honor," she begins. She looks at the flowers for a few moments and then thrusts them back at Rachel. "However, I can't accept it."

Murmurs and gasps ripple through the crowd of campers.

"What are you doing?" Emmy hisses, staring up at the stage. Her fists are clenched tightly at her side.

Meg looks into the crowd, toward her sister. "I violated the Hollyhock Handbook and because of that, someone took the blame for something they didn't do." She moves her eyes toward me. "Sorry, Abigail."

Meg turns to face Hock-Eye, who is deep in conversation with Rachel at the corner of the stage. "Sorry, Hock-Eye, for not telling you sooner." Meg squints back into the spotlight. "And sorry, Camp Hollyhock, for disappointing you." Then she turns and runs across the stage.

The crowd of campers begin to buzz among themselves. Hock-Eye puts the bullhorn up to her lips. "Mary Elizabeth!" she shouts. Meg turns around at the edge of the stage. "Meet me in my office in five minutes and bring your sister." Meg nods and races down the steps and out the barn door.

Emmy and I run after her. We find her leaning against

the wooden fence that surrounds the field where we competed in the Hollympics. Those games seem like such a long time ago. The moon is full and bright, shining like a giant light bulb in the sky.

"What the heck?" Emmy yells, throwing her hands up in the air. "Nobody ever gives up the Hollyhock Honor. And nobody admits to violating the Hollyhock Handbook! You are going to get in so much trouble."

"And so are you," Meg says.

Emmy puts her hands on her hips.

"I'm telling Hock-Eye what you did," Meg adds.

"What?" Sofia calls as she flies toward us. Gabby, Rachel, and Quinn are jogging a few feet behind her. Sofia stops next to me and puts her hands on her knees while she catches her breath. "What did Emmy do?"

"She's the one who broke Rachel's phone," Meg says.

"Stop talking!" Emmy shouts.

"No!" Meg says. "I'm tired of taking your advice."

The rest of Clovis Cabin joins Sofia and me at the fence. Quinn, Gabby, Sofia, Rachel, and I form a small semicircle around the two sisters.

"You might as well give up, Emmy," Rachel says. "Abigail and I saw the photo of you on my phone. We know you stole it."

Emmy stomps over to Rachel. Even though she's our counselor and older than us, she still has to look up to glare at Rachel in the eyes. "I wasn't stealing it, I was confiscating it," Emmy says. "I was going to take it to Hock-Eye and report you."

"You had no right—" Rachel says.

Emmy interrupts her. "You had no right stealing the Hollyhock Honor from me last year! I was going to be the first camper in Hollyhock history to win three in a row."

"I didn't steal it," Rachel protests. "I won it."

Emmy plants her hands on her hips. "Violators of the Hollyhock Handbook don't deserve honors. And I wasn't going to let you get away with it this year."

"So why didn't you ever report Rachel to Hock-Eye?" Quinn asks.

"Because she tripped over the chair in the common room and broke the phone," I say. "She knew Rachel would blame her for breaking it, and she would have to replace it. But Emmy, my question is why did you sneak into our cabin to take the phone? You could have simply confronted Rachel about it and demand she hand it over. Then none of this would ever have happened."

Meg throws her arms up. "That's exactly what I told her

to do!" she yells. "But *nooooo*, Emmy said she had a better plan that would take Rachel by surprise. She always has to do everything her way."

"Sounds like Emmy should have listened to her sister," I say.

"Wait," Quinn says, pointing at Emmy. "*You're* Meg's sister?"

Emmy nods.

"The super amazing one that always knows exactly what to do in every situation?" Sofia asks.

"Present situation excluded," I add.

"But Meg, you said your sister's name was Madeline," Gabby says.

"It is," I explain. "Her full name is Madeline Elise George, but she goes by her first two initials, *M* and *E*. Emmy."

Sofia puts her hands to her temples and then fans out her fingers like fireworks. "Mind. Blown!" she says. "How come you never told us you guys were sisters?"

"I didn't want anyone to know," Meg says. "I get tired of being Meg, the little sister of the super amazing Emmy George. I made Emmy promise not to tell anyone at camp we were sisters. The only person who knew was Hock-Eye. For my first year at Hollyhock, I wanted to be just Meg for once, and do camp my way, with no help or advice."

Emmy smirks. "Look how well that turned out. Now we're both in for it. We might not be able to come back next year."

"That's fine with me," Meg says. "I'd rather go to a camp that's never heard of you. After what you've done this week—all the stealing, planting evidence, framing Abigail, and then forcing me to take the blame—I'm ashamed that people even know you're my sister now."

Emmy covers her mouth with her hand.

Meg pushes herself off the fence. "C'mon. We better not make Hock-Eye wait. We're already in enough trouble as it is." As she trudges through the grass, she stops in front of me. "Abigail, I just want to say again how sorry I am."

I pat her on the shoulder. "No need for more apologies. I've already forgiven you. It's a natural instinct for you to protect someone inside your family herd."

Meg looks back at her sister. "My instincts were wrong."

Emmy clenches her fists at her side. As she marches back to the cabins, she shoves her way through our little semicircle of friends.

"Hey," Meg yells at her. "You better apologize to Abigail and Rachel too. Or I'll tell Hock-Eye how you broke into our cabin *twice*. Once to steal the phone and again to plant it in Abigail's stuff. You definitely will be banned from Hollyhock for life for that!"

Emmy freezes. She groans and slowly turns around. "Sorry, Rachel and Abigail." She swings back around and follows her sister. As she disappears into the dark, we can hear Emmy's boots tramp along the trail.

"I would *not* have predicted that," Quinn says.

"When did you figure out they were sisters, Abigail?" Gabby asks.

"Actually just a few minutes ago," I explain. "They were standing right next to each other and I noticed how similar they looked. I can't believe none of us noticed before now. And also, Emmy took a selfie with Rachel's phone before she broke it. In the picture was a blue plaid water bottle with the initials *MEG*."

Sofia snaps her fingers. One of her sparkles flashes in the moonlight. "Oh yeah, it was on the floor that night of the break in."

"Emmy must have left it there when she snuck in the window," I say. "To cover for her sister, Meg just said it was hers."

Rachel links her elbow into mine. "See, I told you everything would work out the way it was supposed to."

Huckleberries and Hollyhockers start filing out of the barn. The Huckleberries trudge to a yellow school bus parked by the barn. The Hollyhockers set out on the path to the cabins. We all head toward Clovis, Rachel's arm still linked with mine.

Gabby nods as we walk. "Now it's making sense why you guys so easily forgave Meg. You both knew she didn't do it."

"I'm surprised Abigail would allow her to take the fall like that," Quinn says. "She's such a stickler for protocol." Her wink signals to me that she's making fun of me, which, in true ODB fashion, is a signal that she indeed feels fondness for me. I link my elbow to hers. She smiles and hooks her elbow with Gabby's, who walks on the other side of her.

"Hey, Quinn," Sofia says as she links her arm with Gabby. "I heard you broke up with Jason."

"My sources say yes," Quinn says.

"I told you he was too short for you," Gabby adds.

As we head down the path to Clovis Cabin arm in arm, the frogs tune their croaks, readying themselves for tonight's symphony.

"So Jason wasn't the right guy for Quinn," Sofia says. "What else have we learned this week?"

"Don't bring your phone to camp," says Rachel.

Everyone laughs.

"The answer that you seek is sometimes the opposite of what you think," Quinn says.

"*Ooooh,* that's a super good one," Gabby says. "You should put that in the Coot."

She turns to look to Sofia. "And I totally mean that, by the way."

"I wasn't going to say a thing," Sofia says. "In fact, I totally agree with you."

"Yeah, right," Gabby says.

"What?" Sofia says. "I can be nice too." She nudges Gabby. "I've learned from the best."

"Well, I've learned that friendship is not an exact science," I say.

Rachel leans her head against mine. "You can thank me later for teaching you that one," she says.

As we all walk arm-in-arm to Clovis Cabin, it suddenly occurs to me that not just one but two girls are invading my personal space on either side of me, and I don't feel the least bit squirmy or uncomfortable. For once I'm not thinking about lice, germs, or bacteria.

I let out a long breath of air. I've done it. I've made a friend. I look back and forth down at the line of girls. Perhaps five friends. I'm not like the noble gas helium after all. I can mingle with the other fun elements around me. And I am indeed happy.

Jennifer Orr

Jennifer Orr is a writer and former elementary school librarian. She lives in Walnut Creek, California, with her husband and two daughters. She has never kissed a banana slug.